ABOUT THE AUTHOR

Ann Bailey was born in the U.K., lived six years in Singapore, and is resident in The Netherlands. Her hobbies are Writing, Current Affairs and playing 'Bridge'.

"Leaves in the Tea" is a sequel to "An Innocent cup of Tea" and she hopes to complete a Trilogy next year.

www.annbailey.info

Order this book online at www.trafford.com
or email orders@trafford.com

Most Trafford titles are also available at major online book retailers.

Photograph: Claire Majoor

Printed in the United States of America.

ISBN: 978-1-4907-0709-9 (sc)
ISBN: 978-1-4907-0708-2 (e)

Trafford rev. 10/24/2013

 www.trafford.com

North America & international
toll-free: 1 888 232 4444 (USA & Canada)
fax: 812 355 4082

LEAVES IN THE TEA

ANN BAILEY

To
Alan and Shirley

Dear Reader,
I have tried to include the storyline
of my first novel, "An Innocent Cup of
Tea", in this sequel. I hope I have been
successful.

WILL and ROSIE

Will WINDSOR HAD JOGGED passed Emily Nielson many times as she walked her dog across the heath. They had vaguely nodded until their casual greetings broadened out into trivial small talk. Finally, an old weathered park bench, overlooking converging paths and known locally as the 'Crossing', became their meeting place.

His desire for her was inevitable. How could he not fall for her and he hoped she was, at the very least, impressed by his wit and humour. He thought shared humour led to a special kind of friendship, possibly a special kind of love.

He had not told Emy where he lived or that he was living with Rosie though, later, he learnt they knew each other through Rosie's meditation group. He also learnt that Emy visited Rosie from time to time but, curiously, he was never home when she did. He thought Rosie did not want him around when the mostly troubled members of her club came to coffee or tea. He had taken the easy way out and not offered Emy any unnecessary information and she did not ask him, although she chattered rather openly about her own family.

Now, it seemed impossible that he would never see her again walking towards him with her small poodle jumping through the heather, never discuss life and love and whatever else came to mind. It seemed impossible that he would never be able to stroll or jog across the heath without any hope of meeting her. She had been so alive, so present. Now she was gone, forever gone.

He thought warmly of the morning she had asked him home for coffee. He had readily accepted and was disloyal to Rosie. He could not regret his morning of passion, how could he when he had desired her for months, fantasized kissing her, touching her, making love to her.

Some weeks later, he had come home from a difficult meeting with the bank manager to find Rosie clearing up the coffee cups in the kitchen.

"Had a visitor?", he had asked, casually.

"Yes, your big friend, Mrs. Nielson, I believe you know each other rather well", she answered, banging a tray too hard on a worktop

"Do I know a Mrs. Nielson?".

"The helpless little woman you meet on the heath".

"Who?".

"Don't play games".

"Oh, Emy Nielson. But you also know her".

"Perhaps you know her even better".

"Shouldn't think so", he replied, putting the cups in the washing up water hoping to defuse the situation. "She takes her dog for a walk", he replied, now on the defence.

"Listen, Will, it's becoming obvious".

"We're only talking".

"Why is it you men are always attracted by the 'poor little me' strategy", she shouted, angrily.

"That's not true, Rosie. That's unfair".

"Listen, she is obviously unhappy but, at the end of the day, it's got nothing to do with us. I think we need to sort things out, clarify our position so to speak. Don't you agree?".

He looked at her with affection, he had hurt her and he was sorry for that. She was his best friend and always would be. He wanted to say that changing her surname would not change anything. He would not love her more than he did now, as he had always done.

"And?", she added, aggressively.

"Tell me what you would like me to say and I will say it. You deserve better than me", he added, sounding a little insincere.

"That's probably true but you'll do for the time being. Agreed?".

"Agreed. Would you like me to make another pot of coffee?".

Her voice softened. "Yes, do that".

"And afterwards", he smiled, lovingly.

"I can't think of anything else I would rather do", she murmured, her eyes glistening softly with love and forgiveness.

A few weeks later he found Emy drinking tea with Rosie. Luckily, Emy had covered up her surprise as Rosie announced their impending marriage. Their conversation had become jokey through the inevitable tension and Emy made an excuse that she could not stay long. Rosie had stood with her head slightly to one side as though to say, 'now we've got that out of the way'. He had left the room feeling miserable, if not reprimanded.

He had met Emy just once more on the heath. Now he wished he had treasured the precious minutes they had together as they followed the small paths. She talked mostly about Jack who had just returned from one of his midlife 'freedom trips', though she did not know how long he would stay. She went on to tell him how her friend, Helen, had been chasing Jack for years. Jack had said there was nothing between them which she thought unlikely and, actually, she did not want to know. He had vaguely listened to her worries and finally suggested she should, perhaps, ask Helen to tell the truth which he thought was even more unlikely.

Then he told Emy how Rosie wanted to marry in the old chapel which had originally been a small outbuilding attached to the house. It had been blessed, a century ago, by a religious splinter group and had flourished for a while until the congregation dwindled to a couple of old people and then to none. It had stayed a chapel though no one knew when the last Service had been held or even by whom. He had suggested marrying in a registry office but Rosie was adamant and, after a heated discussion, he agreed to the chapel and Rosie vaguely agreed to putting the house up for sale when they returned from their short honeymoon.

They had walked in silence as he envisaged the sombre place offering Calvinistic austerity, stone altar, a crude Cross, two candlesticks, stone floor, pews straight and unforgiving to the back and two coloured glass windows, A heavy wooden door led to a gravel path in the garden which Rosie's mother had insisted was to be left open every day so that those looking for spiritual comfort, or even just a rest, could sit there for a while. He could only assume the place held some kind of sentimental value for he could not think of any other reason why Rosie would want to marry there.

"Now she's gone. Gone, just like that", he murmured, turning his thoughts back to Emy and how Jack and Helen had saved her from drowning only to leave her alone while they lunched. She was dead when Jack went to check up on her, an unnecessary death from secondary drowning. His anger at their stupidity, carelessness, ignorance, returned and he closed his eyes and let the pain overwhelm him. He did that once in a while, accept the loss, accept the pain as he relived the time he had known her. He had loved Emy and lost her.

He controlled his frustration by thinking of Rosie. She had been in his life since he was a small boy, she was his soul mate and lover, had welcomed him home at the end of a field trip, welcomed him into her kitchen and bed. As Rosie always said, they were comparable to an old pair of comfortable slippers. He always smiled when he thought of her.

*

He and Rosie married as she had wanted, the chapel was decorated with summer flowers and garlands of red and white roses fell across the altar. The choice of colours puzzled him for, as far as he knew, red and white flowers stood for blood and even death. He wondered if Rosie knew that or maybe the superstition was outdated.

The local priest had blessed their rather old union and he had kissed the bride as expected. They were about to walk back down the aisle when, suddenly, Rosie pulled herself up onto the altar and waved her bouquet while she did a small dance. He had laughed and clapped with the guests, while the priest played down any feelings he might have harboured in his spiritual breast. He had, lovingly, lifted Rosie off the stone slab and led her back down the aisle while the guests continued to clap and cheer. He thought everyone had seen it as Rosie's day of glory for which she had waited far too long.

They had an offer for their house far quicker than expected. A retired couple had fallen in love with what they called the 'original features'. Rosie had cried and told him she could never leave her family home and he had spent weeks trying to persuade her why they had to, how he could no longer afford the heating bills and the upkeep. In fact, he had never been able to afford them and their burden would disappear with the stroke of a pen.

She had refused to be reasonable and he had firmly held her arm and pointed to the high ceilings, the stone floor which led from the vestibule through the hall to the kitchen and scullery. Ice cold areas which were not to heat in the winter. Not to mention the sash windows which were constantly jammed, the creaking staircase, the huge hot water boiler in the bathroom, the temperamental central heating boiler and the damp basement All these things pressed down on him, depressed him, made him want to run away whereas they could be solved.

He had walked angrily out of the house and onto the heath and sat now for the first time, in what seemed ages, on the bench at the 'Crossing'. He closed his eyes, imagining Emy might suddenly appear in the distance, hastening her step when she saw him waiting for her. He could not believe she would never come again, laugh at his jokes which blended with her own dry humour, deep discussions over religion, politics and the world at large, including love. 'To love', she had said, 'was to suffer'. Now he suffered a pain, the pain mourners suffer.

He turned his thoughts back to his youth and the first time he had come to 'Tower Lodge', a rambling house with an equally rambling garden.

His father, who was called Reginald, had already divorced his mother who he remembered as a bright, jingling, jangling, woman. Their marriage had lasted ten years and then, he supposed in a hopeless well of desperation, his mother left him and his father for a car salesman. He had to admit he sold sports cars. He could sympathise with his mother as he grew older though he never really forgave her for abandoning him. Everyone said that opposites got on well together but he thought that was a 'load of codswallop' for Reginald had been a precise, dominant, man, his hair perfectly parted and sleekly combed. He was slightly built, immaculately dressed, polished his black shoes every night before he went to bed and wore a pair of gold rimmed glasses. He was an accountant, a man of his time.

His very strict and rather bullying father had told him that Stella, the owner of 'Tower Lodge', was the nicest woman he had ever met and she was going to be his new mother, since his real one had other interests, and he would have a sister called Rosie.

Later, he had learnt how his father and Stella had met over a sandwich lunch, in a rather mediocre café, and that Stella worked part time in a library not far from his office. Her husband, who had been much older than she was, had died leaving her a large house, no other capital and a small child.

Reginald had comforted the widow, Stella, and before long had moved in with her which was a solution to her financial difficulties and, perhaps, a good investment for him in the future, if he could lay his hands on her house, if he could persuade her to marry him. After all, he insisted, living together was living in sin. However, Stella was a broadminded woman, not of her day, and refused to get bogged down in the ensuing paperwork. A Marriage Certificate.

However, Reginald moving in with Stella was his saving. Her daughter, Rosie, was two years younger than he was and Stella was a warm and loving woman. He had luck to have landed in this family and forgot his mother rather quickly.

Two years later, he was sent to boarding school which he surprisingly enjoyed. Rosie stayed home and, because she was shy and insecure, it was decided to leave her in the local school. In any case, Stella wanted her child near to her, she loved her, she was all she had and was not about to hand her over to some institute. He liked Stella immensely, certainly more than his father who he disliked just as immensely.

*

He had been in his second year studying archaeology when Stella telephoned him to say Reginald had disappeared for some considerable time, in fact three months. He had, of course, asked her whether she had reported him missing to which she replied that she had been forced to do so, seeing how his office insisted on it. His father had been suspended from work until he returned, hopefully with a satisfactory reason though she could not think of one herself.

He had been astounded for his father was not an impulsive man, rather the opposite.

"I can't believe it", he had said.

"I know, I can't either, but he has. He's taken all his clothes except for his dark suits and briefcase. It looks as though he wants to start a new life".

"Who with?".

"No idea".

"I'll come down tomorrow".

"No need", Stella replied. "You can't do anything, wait until the end of term".

Stella had seemed only slightly depressed when he arrived. Reginald had indeed packed a suitcase with his most informal clothes, which were rather limited, together with his passport, wallet, cheque book, gold watch, gold pen and a pair of spare glasses.

The police had done their best to trace him but they had only found his car, with the keys still in the ignition, parked somewhere outside Dover. It had been thoroughly examined for foul play but only his and Stella's fingerprints had been found and they had drawn a blank. They had concluded that Reginald had met someone, left the car, and driven away with whoever it was. They had no reason to think otherwise and Reggie became another one of many thousands of missing people who might, or might not, resurface.

Stella thought he had probably taken off to the Continent though there was no trace that he had done so. Still he was a quiet man and Stella reckoned no one really knew anyone.

His work had taken him away from home and he had felt a degree of sadness every time he left to go on some 'dig' for he not only loved Stella but also Rosie who had turned out to be incredibly beautiful. Her long hair was a mass of curls, her eyes bright blue, her skin almost translucent and she dressed in a sort of bohemian style. Whenever he saw a field of flowers, he thought of Rosie running through it, her slim body almost discernible under her thin cotton dress, her blonde hair flying in a light breeze. She was for him the personification of beauty. He had, unwillingly, hidden his feelings for he could not imagine she would ever be interested in a stepbrother who had teased her when she could not keep up with him.

But Rosie, who had always giggled and flashed her eyes at him, had changed. She seemed to ignore him and he felt hurt because somehow he had always been close to her, shared silly secrets, climbed trees, cycled to a stream a little further from their house, fished for tiddlers and cooked potatoes in a fire. Everything which made an idyllic childhood. He could not understand what had changed between them, he was the same, he had not changed, not that he knew.

He had expected to hear how Rosie had a steady boyfriend, was engaged or getting married. But every time he came home she was still drawing and painting and writing. Stella said there had been interested young men but Rosie had brushed them aside, though she was sure the right one would eventually come along. He had wanted to shout, "I'm the right one", but he held back in case he might be instantly rebuffed.

He had gone on to make a short disastrous marriage with an assistant to a college bursar and lesbian. Rosie had found it amusing which, on reflection, actually was. Then Stella had suddenly died of a stroke which left both he and Rosie devastated though her death confirmed that she and Reginald had never married. He and Rosie had both sighed with relief for it simplified the testament. Stella had generously left the house to both of them which seemed to please Rosie because she said he could help with any future upkeep while it gave him a permanent pied à terre. He thought Stella had somehow tied them together even if it was only through property.

He had expected Rosie to be lonely when he left on long field trips but she said the old rambling house had been in the family for years and she wanted to stay. It was full of memories. He had accepted her decision because he felt the same but he did not believe she would stay there alone for very long.

"Rosie", he had said, thoughtfully. "You aren't my stepsister. In fact you never were. We are two unrelated, single, people living alone together".

She had laughed at the idea. He loved her.

*

It had been Christmas and Rosie had done her best to make a turkey dinner, which was rather underdone, and a cake. He had appreciated her efforts and they had sat together by a roaring fire in the lounge. Eventually, they had gone upstairs together and he had lain next to her and slowly, carefully, made love. He was surprised when he realised she was not a virgin and decided that her brief engagement to a Belgian school teacher had been more sexual than he had wanted to admit. Anyway, the Belgian had returned to the small country he called home and he was thankful that he had done so. He still shuddered at his disastrous marriage and the idea of Rosie living alone, without him, on the Continent. Then, suddenly, it occurred to him that Rosie had broken her engagement at almost the same time as his divorce. He wondered if that had been coincidental or whether Rosie had been waiting for him, as he had for her.

He had intended marrying Rosie but she had put her finger over his lips and said it was alright as it was. She said that maybe marriage might spoil the magic of their love.

He had not been entirely happy but he had accepted her decision, after all he had one notch in his belt and he could not afford to make another mistake, though he thought Rosie could never be a mistake. He would ask her again, sometime later.

He turned his thoughts back to the present and decided to ignore Rosie for a while to see if she would change her mind, if she would get round to his way of thinking, to accept the generous offer for the house and be rid of it and its ability to swallow any money they might have.

A common white butterfly fluttered around him as he stood up to leave. He thought of Emy.

Rosie seemed unperturbed by his coolness and finally, in a rage, he had shouted at her and called her selfish, something he had never done before. She sighed deeply and replied that he would be happier not to know the why's and wherefore's which made him shout even harder for her resilience was insufferable. He threatened to leave her, she could have the house for all he cared and she would never see him again.

Tears formed in Rosie's eyes and he wanted to hold her, comfort her, tell her he would never leave her, but instead he stamped upstairs and pulled a suitcase from out of a cupboard and began to pack.

When he looked up Rosie was standing in the doorway. It seemed to him that she grew lovelier as she grew older, her hair was still the mass of long curls though a little thinner now and the lines around her eyes made her look even softer, tender, more loving.

He sat on the bed and she stood in front of him and held his head against her body.

"You are all I have, ever had. I loved you from the moment we met", she whispered.

"Then why, Rosie. We could have a lovely life together. Why hang onto this old place. Why?".

Rosie sighed. "Because of what happened".

"What happened?".

"No one else can live here".

"Why, why can't anyone else live here?".

"You can't guess?".

"No, what must I guess?".

Rosie sat on the bed next to him sobbing, hot tears rolled down her ruddy cheeks and her curls stuck against her face which she tried to wipe aside with her sleeve. She drew her breath in as she spoke.

"Your father. He never left, he's still here. He's in the chapel", she managed to whisper, her voice breaking up between light wails.

"What are you talking about?", he eventually managed to gasp as a feeling of deep apprehension flowed through him, stifling him, so he could hardly answer her.

"He is in the chapel, behind the altar. I'm so sorry, I'm so sorry".

He wished he could assimilate what she was saying, wished she had not said it, wished he had just accepted it all as it was.

Rosie bent over, her head in her hands, as she told him how his father had attacked her, raped her, in the chapel. How her mother was at the local hairdresser's and not expected to return for some time but when she arrived at the shop it was closed as the hairdresser's daughter had been taken ill.

Her mother had heard her screaming when she returned and, in horror, had picked up a brass candlestick and hit Reginald on the head with it. She spoke quickly, stuttering, as she tried to explain what happened.

She had sat with her mother at the kitchen table and eventually persuaded her that what she had done was understandable, a normal human reaction, and she did not see why Reginald should spoil their lives. Why tell anyone, why have the social services across the floor, police investigations, court hearings, all the dirt spread across the local and even the national newspapers and, not least, poor Will. The humiliation and pain he would suffer, perhaps he would leave and never return. Neither of them could bear that.

She had suggested hiding Reginald under the stones in the chapel where he would be nearer to God. Anyway, moving him would only leave a trail of evidence. Her mother had thought the stones would be too heavy for them so she had suggested asking Uncle Henry, her mother's brother, to help because she did not believe he would let his sister be arrested for manslaughter, or even a more terrible crime.

They had discussed the matter at length, her mother being unsure whether Henry would be prepared to go to such lengths for her, while she assured her that it was the best solution to an insolvable problem.

Eventually, her mother had agreed that Henry would most probably help since he hated Reginald and would, most likely, be extremely sympathetic to his long suffering sister.

Henry had stayed a few days with them, telling his wife how he needed to help Stella since Reginald had gone off, probably with some woman, and how Stella said that Reginald was sexually overactive and his disappearance did not particularly surprise her. She had expected something of the sort. They would just wait and see whether his fling was to be short lived and perhaps he would come home with his tail between his legs, so to speak. His wife promised not to tell anyone and hoped he could be of comfort to his sister and Rosie.

Henry had thought it better if they removed the stone paving behind the altar and dig deep enough to bury Reginald in a sitting position, since the less stones removed the better.

They had carefully shovelled the sandy earth into heavy plastic bags, making sure that no surrounding stones were chipped or damaged. In fact, the exercise was far more difficult than they had anticipated for the hole had to be made wider as it became deeper.

Eventually, Henry thought the hole was good enough to place Reginald in it with his back leaning against one side and his feet against the other. Then they brushed his hair, placed his glasses on his nose, his spare ones in his pocket along with his gold pen, wallet, cheque book, bank pass and passport. They checked to see his gold watch was still on his wrist before they bent him over as far as possible, said a small prayer and threw the sandy earth back over him. They thought he had everything he needed in another world, only he was sitting around in this one probably feeling very bored.

Henry then replaced the stones, hammering them down gently, rather professionally, with a special hammer made for that purpose. The floor was brushed clean and, since there was no cement between the stones, he hoped the disturbed sand would quickly blend in with the rest.

"Don't tell anyone he's missing until you have to", Henry had warned them. "The stones have first to settle and please if you get caught keep me out of it. Just say the two of you did it alone. It is possible you could have done it. So please shut up and for God's sake stay in this house until after I've died. In fact, until you are both taken out between six planks".

They had sworn before the simple wooden Cross that they would do that and never divulge their secret. Not to anyone.

Her mother had packed Reginald's casual clothes into a suitcase, removed all makers' names and a dry cleaning tag from his linen jacket and filled the case with stones.

When it was dark, she and her mother drove to a deep fast flowing river and threw the suitcase over the bridge. They had held hands as they watched bubbles form as it disappeared and sighed with relief as they walked away.

They reckoned if the suitcase or clothes were found then tracing them back to Reginald would be almost impossible.

Next day, Stella drove Reginald's car to Dover, left it on a lonely picnic area, and driven back home with Henry who then drove home to his wife.

Will sat dumbfounded, shaking his head as the story unfolded. Eventually, he said he found Rosie and Stella very brave and Reginald had deserved what he had got. If he had been there he would probably have done the same. Though he was not entirely sure that was so.

He frowned. "But why did you want to marry in the Chapel?".

"I suppose it was a sort of revenge, dance on his grave. He stole my best years, we lived in fear in case we were found out. I think it killed mum. I finally decided to tie the knot when you and Emy were chasing behind each other. And, then, you wanted to sell the house, so I had to tell you".

He sympathised as he held Rosie in his arms.

"You should have told me. Now I understand why you didn't want to marry all those years ago and why you didn't want to have a family. You poor thing. But your Belgian fiancé?".

"Yes, life was fragile. And André? I couldn't go through with it and I wanted to make you jealous".

"You did that and you also dug yourselves into a hole but luckily not that one. Reginald is the toad in the hole", he laughed, nervously.

"Yes", agreed Rosie. "But there's just one small problem. Henry is in a Care Home. He's dement. I went to see him a few months ago and to my horror, in front of a nurse, he asked if Reginald was still sitting in the chapel.

It seems that, once in a while, he can still remember something from long ago. I thought I would die, the nurse ignored him but what if he tells them he buried Reginald behind the altar. What if the Care Home tells the police?".

"Yes, that could be a problem". He considered the situation. "There are two options, as I see it. Either hope for the best or dig him up and bury him somewhere else. I think that's the best".

"I agree. We will have to make sure we have all the bones, if we leave even one behind and the police find it, then we're in trouble".

"Don't forget I'm an archaeologist".

"Yes, of course, I forgot that".

"And then we can sell the house?".

"The very next day", Rosie agreed, elated that she had shared her secret and would be able to put Reginald to rest at last.

"Rosie", he asked, softly. "Is that why Stella left me half the house, she thought perhaps she owed me something?".

"I don't know. But I do know she loved you. She saw you as her own son, perhaps that was her way of keeping us together".

Will found he had to dig deeper than he had anticipated since the bones seemed to have sunk into the sandy earth and the hole became wider as he dug further. He had found the skull almost immediately and had held it up, rather like Hamlet did Yorick's, and studied it as though it was just another relic on some field expedition in some god forsaken place.

"Yes, he got quite a hit".

"Sorry, he was your father", Rosie murmured, standing on the edge of the hole with a container bag, grimacing as each bone fell upon the last, while Will tried to convince himself that his father deserved his fate. "After all", she murmured, "he could have landed up in prison and, at least, he was buried in a chapel which is as good as it gets".

"Doesn't matter. I could never get on with him. He was a tight fisted bastard. I think he sent me to boarding school just to get me out of the way".

"You're right about that".

He stopped digging and looked up.

"He was around me for years. Passing too close to me, touching my breasts by so-called accident. I said I would tell my mother, but he told me I would be hurting her and she had a nice life and he would give me anything I wanted. I told him I didn't want anything from him".

"What a creep. You poor thing".

"It's a long time ago, I've put it behind me".

"You've had a bad time, Rosie dear, carrying such a burden alone". He climbed out of the hole and kissed her "I'll make it up to you", he promised. "Don't worry, we'll have this settled by tomorrow and then we'll put the house back on the market".

*

They were almost finished when someone banged on the locked door.

"Mrs. Windsor, Rosie, are you there?".

"Oh, my God, it's that Carter woman. What do we do?", Rosie whispered, almost hysterically.

"Get rid of her, don't let her in for God's sake".

Rosie walked to the large chapel door and squeezed out onto the garden path, closing it behind her as she did so.

"Whatever are you doing?", asked the woman noticing Rosie's dirty hands.

She paused for a second. "Oh, Will and I are going to replace the chapel floor".

"Why do you want to do that?".

"Because", she said, slowly, while her thoughts raced for a reason. "Because we thought we would bring the chapel into the house to open up the hall".

"What a good idea. Can my Ben help you?".

"No, thanks. Absolutely not, we'll give you a ring if we need any help. Nice of you to offer".

"Well, you know where we are if you need us. What a good idea", she repeated.

Will 'phoned a stone mason offering him a good quality flagstone floor together with three slabs of stones which were the altar. The mason was keen and said he would be around the next day to have a look. He explained that the stones had still to be lifted off the ground but they were not cemented in. He casually mentioned that he had begun the work himself but had found the stones too heavy for him to lift. The stone mason told him not to worry. It was all in a day's work.

Will looked down at where he had removed the stones, "I'm going to have to lift more. I can hardly say I started by the altar. I'll begin in a corner and make it look as though I've made my way up to here", he puffed through his lips at the thought of the work ahead and his backache which was worsening by the day.

"Can I help?".

"No, just make dinner, I'll either drop dead from stress or I would have worked up an appetite. I don't know which one it is yet. What a bloody mess this is".

"Actually, there was very little blood", Rosie, remarked, thoughtfully.

"Thank God for small mercies", he muttered.

The mason seemed rather pleased with the floor and the price he had paid for it. Removing the stones had not been a problem and he really did not understand why anyone would want to replace them. For him, stones were the centre of the universe, they were his work, his hobby, his life. He saw them as other men saw a woman's body but, unlike a woman, they never changed their shape unless he wished it.

Rosie giggled and Will said he had never thought of stones in that way.

Later, Will pulled a sports bag full of Regie's bones from under his bed where he had hidden it after his 'dig'.

"Where's the best place to lay him out?", he asked, sounding worried.

Rosie thought for a moment. "No one goes to the tower, not unless I take them there".

"Good thinking, I'll start now", he answered, as he made his way to his study to sort out his field bag.

He was busy brushing off the excess earth from Reginald's bones when Rosie arrived with a cup of coffee.

"He had a bit of arthritis. I reckon Stella saved him a lot of pain".

"Well, that's something", Rosie replied, trying to sound positive.

"I think we're missing a small bone from his right foot and a couple of teeth. You don't happen to know if he lost any teeth, do you?".

"No idea. Never looked in his mouth".

"You can be happy for that", he laughed, now beginning to find the exercise even more bizarre than he had anticipated. "I'll have to dig again but, first, I want to visit my mother, I haven't seen her for ages, perhaps she can shed some light on his missing teeth. I think it's time to hear her out, she's just moved to a small flat down by the coast".

"Now you can introduce me as your wife".

He smiled, lovingly. "Yes, I can do that now".

"You should go more often".

"I never know what to talk about", he complained. "What can I say to her after all these years. We have nothing in common".

"She's your mother. She's old, you can afford to be kind".

"I'll see what I can do", he mumbled, turning away so Rosie could not see him gripping his teeth at the thought of a long overdue visit.

*

Poppy, real name Petronella, was still as bubbly as he remembered her on the occasional visits he had made over the years. Her now thin blonde hair was frizzy from too much peroxide and too many 'perms'. Her lips were streaked with a bright red lipstick which seemed unable to find the outline of her rather indefinable lips.

She welcomed her child with open arms, forgetting he was middle aged and not the ten year old she had forsaken. He placed his arms around her frail body and gently rubbed her back while she smudged his summer jacket with makeup and black tears from her mascara painted eye lashes.

She eventually pulled back. "You never come", she almost whispered. "I am so lonely, I have no one, only you, and you don't want to know me".

"That's not true, Mum", he replied, looking uncomfortable as he lied. "It's just that I have been so busy. I want to ask you a few things. I want to get it all sorted out before it's too late".

"Before I die".

"Yes, to be honest. There are so many loose ends, things you have never told me about

Reginald".

"Reggie?", she questioned, suddenly sitting up and looking a lot stronger. "What about him?".

"I want to know why you left him".

"He was the meanest sod I have ever known. He was older than me, I was only twenty and pregnant when I married him. He took my money and gave me so much per week and I had to write down exactly on what and where I had spent it. Meanwhile, he bought anything he wanted for himself".

Will sat upright as though to defend himself.

"And me then. You left me with him. Was he worth more than me?".

"I had already introduced him to Stella and then I made sure they met again just before I was divorced. It was a bit cloak and dagger but it worked. I didn't leave before I was sure their friendship was definite. You see I had to leave you behind. My late husband, Rodney, as sweet as he was, didn't want to get tied down with children. He was always off on some car rally or another. He wanted me but you weren't part of the bargain. So I had to make a choice. I thought that you would have less than ten years with the bastard whereas I might have a lifetime. I believe Rodney loved me and that does not come around very often".

"Don't you think you were a bit selfish?".

"Perhaps, but I knew Stella was a good woman and I did keep an eye on you and when you went to boarding school I knew you would be alright, get a good education, get away from him".

He wanted to shout that she had been a selfish tart and that he despised her and had only come to find out just a little more about Reggie's physical attributes.

He cleared his throat. "I'm doing a study on inherited physical features. Do you happen to know if Reggie ever lost a couple of his molars?", he asked, in a cold controlled voice.

Poppy looked amazed, "I don't think I can remember that. Well, let me see, he did have a couple of wisdom teeth taken out".

"No, not wisdom teeth, other teeth".

"Well, he once told me that his school dentist took a couple of teeth out to make room in his mouth for others to grown straight. The only reason I remember that is because I took you to the dentist and he said he did not think you would ever need to lose any teeth since your mouth was wide enough". She giggled. "Big enough".

"Right, fine, thanks Poppy", he answered, not sharing her joke. "I know enough".

"Are you coming again soon?"

"Whenever I can".

Poppy turned to Rosie. "Your mother and I were such good friends".

"Friends?", queried Rosie, her voice rising a couple of octaves from surprise.

"Of course. If you want to get rid of your husband you must tell your girl friends how unhappily married you are".

"Really", replied Rosie, coldly.

"One of them will always take the bait, if she is single or unhappily married. Guaranteed to work", she giggled. "It worked out well, your mother was looking for a new husband and I had one to spare", she giggled again, closing her now weak eyes as she did so. "Where is Reggie?", she added.

"We don't know. He disappeared long ago, we've never heard from him", Rosie informed her, icily.

"Well, I'm not surprised. Stella wouldn't marry him. She was going to but never did. Your mother saw through him, he was after her house or at least half of her house. He probably found someone else who was more obliging. Though I must say they stayed together for quite some time. Longer than I thought they would", she added.

"We only found out they weren't married after Stella died. Had she married Reggie and had he owned half the house then there would have been a problem settling her testament, since Reggie is missing", Rosie informed her, staring across the room at a photograph of a young couple leaning against a sports car. "You know, Will and I never told anyone we were not stepbrother and sister. Why tell if no one asks".

"Quite right, if you had told them they would only think you were having if off together. Well, it would have been strange if you weren't", Poppy added, laughing.

Rosie sighed. "My mother was not the kind of woman to live with a man. I guess she had too many financial problems".

"Yes, lack of money can be the biggest reason why women tolerate men", sighed Poppy, as though she had her own memories. "Anyway, she saved herself the bother of a divorce. Perhaps he found another widow. Good riddance to him. Poor Stella", she added.

"That's always a possibility", agreed Rosie, smiling at her suggestion.

"Whatever, he's been gone for so long he is probably already dead", Will suggested.

"Maybe he lived in some beautiful villa in South America and had a really good life", added Rosie, enjoying the conversation.

"Sooner or later, he would need to renew his passport", pondered Poppy, frowning as it occurred to her that it was more than likely he was still in the country. "Passports can be a stumbling block", she murmured.

"Well, you can buy anything, if you have enough money", Will replied. "Do you like living down here?", he added, changing the subject.

They stayed longer than they had expected. In fact, Rosie found Poppy rather refreshing, honest. She had wanted to dislike her but somehow could not and she could see Will felt the same way. She thought it would be good for him to see his wayward mother, from time to time, and she was sure that deep down Poppy must feel bad about leaving her child. She decided Will should make it up with his mother, offer the olive branch, before she died.

"Well, Poppy, enjoy the Kent coast", Will said, kindly, giving his mother a warm kiss. "We'll be along as soon as we can, we have just a few things to do".

"You must come for a few days", suggested Rosie. "That's if you want to".

Tears formed in Poppy's eyes. "Do you really mean that, would you have me?".

Rosie felt a lump in her throat. "Of course", she replied, gently. "Why not, then you can see my mother's house".

"Oh, I saw it decades ago. Your mother and I were school friends".

"I never knew that", replied Rosie, rather stunned.

"Has it changed much?".

"Well, that's what we are doing now", Will replied.

Mrs. Carter and her husband, Ben, were standing by the locked chapel door when they arrived home. Agnes stood with her handbag dangling over her stomach while Ben doffed his cap in respect.

"Ah, there you are", she gushed. "Ben and I think we, and the village, owe you so much. All those meetings, meditations and positive thinking, here in the old chapel. Ben says he wants to help you".

"That's most kind of you", replied Will, acknowledging Ben as he stepped forward as though volunteering for some dangerous mission.

"I'm a bricklayer. My boss has a good name

around these parts, I can recommend him, and I can do a bit extra for you".

"Right, I'm sure we can use both of you".

"I've 'eard you want to pull a wall down".

"Well, yes, but I don't think we can do that so easily. It's an outside wall".

"Don't you worry about that. My boss, Mr. Willard, can arrange all of that. Perhaps I can 'ave a look at it?".

"Come in", Will invited, nervously.

"Can you come back at the end of the week", suggested Rosie. "We've been out all day and we want to eat something and have a rest".

"That's fine Mrs. W. Let's say Friday evening after work. I expect my boss will come along".

"Excellent", Will sighed. "Until then".

"Come along Ben, let these poor people have a rest", his wife said, assertively, pulling on his arm.

"I need a drink", Will muttered.

*

He was on the point of climbing out of the newly dug hole, after digging for hours looking for his father's lost bone, when he looked up to see Ben's knees.

"I've just come to say that Mr. Willard will see you Monday afternoon, if that's alright with you. What's that 'ole for?", he added, innocently.

"This hole", Will replied, clearing his throat to give himself time to fantasize, "is for a fountain. We thought we might have one where the altar was".

"Yea", agreed Ben. "That's nice, a door at each end, one to the 'all and the other to the garden. You would see the fountain from the 'all, that's real nice".

"Yes, Rosie and I thought it would bring life into the old place. I thought I would dig out the shape of the fountain and at the same time see what the earth is like".

"Everything is sand around here, I can tell you that now. Not going to be a round pool then?".

"As I've just said, we're experimenting. Rosie thought an oblong shaped pool would be more modern with perhaps some gold fish in it and water plants, or whatever. She is leaning towards a more clean look. I prefer something more classical, goes better with the room, but I guess she will get her way in the end. That's why we are digging it out now. Just to see how it will look".

Rosie appeared at the chapel door.

"I'm just telling Ben how we are going to put a small fountain in here and how you would like a more modern look, a sort of oriental look".

He could see Rosie blush.

"Yes, it will make it seem peaceful, tranquil, add some atmosphere".

"We once went to a Chinese restaurant", recalled Ben. "Nice but I prefers me roast beef and Yorkshire pudding. Can't wait to get that 'ere opened up", he enthused, knocking on the thick wall between the chapel and the hall. "That'll make the place seem bigger, lighter, and the 'all as well. Can't wait to do that".

Will cleared his throat. "Well, if your boss can

arrange all the paper work".

"He'll be right on it, don't you worry. We'll have this finished in no time. My wife will like this. She's been telling everyone in the village 'bout it".

Rosie glanced over to Will who was visibly perspiring, large damp patches showed on his azure blue shirt and he wiped his forehead with a handkerchief already soiled from the sandy earth.

"Thanks, Ben", cooed Rosie. "It's so nice having people like you around. A job shared is a job halved".

"Don't you mean a trouble shared is a troubled halved", Will corrected, sharply.

Rosie looked irritated. "No, I don't mean that. We don't have any troubles, so if you don't mind, I'll leave it as a job shared".

Ben laughed loudly, "Well said, Mrs. W. It's going to be a pleasure digging out that fish pond though I think you've dug deeper than necessary. Don't you worry, we'll have it fixed in no time".

He walked away still laughing as he left the chapel door open behind him.

"Well, we don't have to close the door anymore, the whole village knows what we're doing", he grumbled.

"I see it as a blessing. We can get on with what we're doing and everyone will think it is what it isn't".

"Fine, but we'll be left with a bloody great bill paying for opening up the wall, new floor, fish pond, fountain and God knows what else. We're going the wrong way, Rosie, we are supposed to be pulling the money in not giving it out".

"Perhaps the price of the house will increase when it's finished", she suggested, hopefully.

"I don't even know what we are planning to do, let alone finishing it".

"We are going to make the most marvellous entrance hall to a beautiful house full of original features. The hall will open out into a pure white plastered room, white marble floor, which can be used as a chapel or, with a bit more imagination, into a dance floor or even a casino", she giggled.

"What a good idea. Why didn't I think of that", he answered, sarcastically. "What shall we call it. 'Reggie's Hideaway'. Bar and Dancing facilities".

Rosie grinned broadly. "Something like that. I'll have to think about it".

"Meanwhile", he added. "There's someone in the tower who still needs a permanent home".

Rosie did not seem at all bothered with their predicament, in fact she was becoming more enthusiastic over the idea of a pool with a fountain, potted plants and an extra room. She was even at the stage of planning a wall of windows, glass doors to the garden and windows in the roof. The chapel would become a conservatory. Selling the house had been swept under the carpet while he was left arranging a mortgage with the Bank.

Plans were submitted and passed by the local Council and Will wondered, on a daily basis, how it had got this far. If Agnes Carter had not arrived when she did, if Rosie had not made up the story of replacing the old stone floor, if Ben Carter had not seen the huge trench he had dug out looking for a bone. All 'if's' he thought, as he pondered on Reggie who was now rolled up in a couple of towels in a sports bag in the tower.

*

It was a book on Feng Shui which finally tipped Rosie into the realms of fantasy. The word Bagua was flung around, a compass was found and a Bagua map drawn up. It seemed that the opening to the hall and the doors to the garden were exactly what were required for the energy to flow through or was it for the spirits. He really could not grasp it all.

Rosie spent hours reading and making notes of the correct plants needed and even fish. It seemed to him that Rosie had found her niche in life. He knew she had always been inclined towards alternative thinking, even spirituality, and he had no inclination to contradict her at any stage of the operation. If she was quiet, he was happy.

An oblong pool was dug out and lined. Water dribbled over two large round smooth stones, spiky grasses and flowering plants were pressed into colourful pots filled with the right kind of soil, of course. Expensive fish were gently eased into the well balanced water and dim lights, tucked under the white marble tiles, lit the pool at night.

He had to agree it was all very charming and could only add to the value of the house. In fact, people had already asked if they could have a small peep at the wonders they had achieved and wished they had the space in their houses to do the same.

Rosie had collected a library of Feng Shui books and walked around their rather large, au natural, garden with her trusted friend, the compass. He knew it was a bad sign and had come to hate the round box with its ever swinging needle and realised it would not be long before Rosie would find a corner where Feng Shui, which he now visualised as an unwelcome entity, would feel most at home.

"We need a Feng Shui rockery", Rosie had informed him one afternoon. "The position here is perfect and the energy can pass through the front door, down the hall, across the pool, through the conservatory, out of the glass doors and over the rockery. All this was meant to be", she added.

"Rosie, it will cost thousands".

"Yes, I know but you see it is the kindest thing we can do for poor Reginald. Can you imagine the spiritual peace he will have under the rockery".

He flopped down in a chair in the now colourful conservatory and was overcome with the desire to splash his weary feet in the pool, clouding Shui's water, disturbing the fish and changing the direction of Feng's wind.

Actually, he thought, after he had stilled his worried soul, Reggie under the rockery was not such a bad idea. They would, of course, have to return him to the ground before the work on the rockery could begin and he felt a strange déjà vu feeling pass through him. Was not digging up Reggie the reason why Feng Shui had arrived in the first place. Now Rosie was suggesting they should rebury Reggie so that he might rest forever in Feng Shui's energy field. He wondered whether there was something he was missing, something he did not quite understand. Eventually, he decided not to query Feng Shui let alone question a woman's logic.

Rosie found a Feng Shui expert through the local garden centre and called him in for advice on how to lay the rockery. He was a quiet man, slightly built as was to be expected, probably because of his healthy diet, who implicitly agreed with Rosie's choice of site and obviously admired this pretty middle aged lady in her flowing frocks and sandals.

Arnold Waters, also known as Arnie, seemed very keen on his Rosie and promised to supervise the work since it was really important how the stones were laid and, of course, the choice of plants. Rosie willingly agreed a price with Arnold Waters which staggered him and his bank manager who, nevertheless, seemed quite happy to offer him an even larger loan since their house was collateral.

Will winced, he had not forgotten the reason for this whole exercise and Reggie under the rockery would once again put a damper on selling. After all, a new owner might not like Fen Shui's rockery and dig it up only to find a bag of bones.

He sighed, Reggie's final abode was inevitable for he realised that throwing the silly old sod into a river was not really appropriate. After all, he should show some kind of respect even though he thought Reggie hardly deserved such a nice resting place.

It was Arnold Waters who hit upon the idea of how to make money. His liking of Rosie was sincere enough and perhaps he wanted her around him as much as possible, seeing how the 'ex' Mrs. Waters had thrown a potted plant at him and told him to shove it up his. The last word was left open to their imagination and he had grinned and thought how right she was.

"I was thinking", said Arnold, pointing to a corner in the garden. "You have so much unused land, whether you might consider putting down a green house. You could grow your own plants, even grow biological vegetables, seeing how you have so much space. There is nothing like home grown products".

"We could sell them here and I could do teas in the conservatory", enthused Rosie.

Will closed his eyes as he visualised a board outside the front garden advertising flowers, biological fruit and vegetables, morning coffee and afternoon teas. However, he had not seen Rosie like this for a long time, bubbling enthusiasm, keen, full of ideas. The Rosie from long ago. He felt he owed her for all the misery she had suffered over so many years. Arnold stood with his eyes open, he had found his soul mate, the woman he admired so much had spark, spontaneity, spirituality, adaptability. A jewel hidden in a stuffy old house. He would open up her life and, softly, slowly bring her into his culture, the one his mother had taught him. He felt fate had brought them together and he would be happy just to see her every day and perhaps innocently touch her hand. In fact, any small morsel from the table of admiration would satisfy him.

Will watched it all with an interest which bordered on connivance, as though he was encouraging a 'special' friendship. He knew he could turn Arnold away but he loved Rosie and if he kicked Arnie out then perhaps she would harbour a hidden resentment. He thought there was something odd about Arnie and he wondered if Mrs. Arnie had her own tale to tell. In any case, Rosie's friendship with Arnie was platonic, not like Emy who was looking for love.

"Fine, Arnold, I think we can work something out", he muttered, his thoughts turning back to Emy.

Arnold marked out the position of the rockery which was in line with the conservatory's glass doors. He said it was perfect for the flow of energy and could be appreciated from within the house when the weather was unfavourable.

Will had glanced over to Rosie who seemed to have forgotten about Reggie in the tower, and his lost bone, as she absorbed every word her guru offered.

"Rosie", he said, softly, after Arnie had gone home, "we still have to put you know who to rest".

"I thought we had already decided on the rockery", she replied, as though the deal was done.

"Yes, but I have to clear the ground, dig a hole. What will Arnie say to that. Won't he find it strange if I do that myself?"

"I know, we'll ask Ben to prepare the ground, so to speak. Then we can dig it out a bit deeper, put Reggie in and cover him up".

"I don't know, I feel we're involving too many people".

"Well, it's a bit like 'the bigger the lie, the more it's believed'. No one will think anything, what with Ben and Arnie around and then the gardeners. There's nothing to think about".

"I hope you're right".

"They're coming next Monday".

"Who are?".

"The gardeners. Arnie has organised it for us".

"Is Arnie going to pay for it?".

"Don't be silly".

He turned away, seriously wondering whether he had made a mistake, perhaps running away with Emy would have been simpler after all. He felt he was digging himself into a deep hole alongside Reggie.

Arnie measured the area where the rockery would be placed in great detail. It appeared that the sun played a large part in Feng Shui's energy field and he assured them that the rock plants would grow better there than anywhere else in the garden and, along with the enhancement of the pool and conservatory, would bring a peace and tranquillity into their lives which they had not yet encountered. Will wondered how he could be privy to such information about their personal lives.

Ben was summoned to clear the area and, just in case it was necessary, to dig a little deeper so that the rocks would have a good foundation.

"You's got something about digging 'oles", he laughed.

"Looks like it", Rosie chirped in. "You and Agnes must come soon, when the weather is a bit brighter and have tea with us. I was actually thinking about opening up the conservatory and having a little tea room. You know when people have walked with their dogs across the heath, they might just like to have a cup of tea or coffee along with scones and cakes", she smiled, sweetly. "Of course, people will have to know we are here. I don't see how I could advertise. Word of mouth is always the best. I suppose, if it were to become popular, I might even have to get a catering licence. Don't you think that's a nice idea, Ben?".

Ben grinned knowingly. "I'll tell Agnes. She knows just about everybody".

"That's what I was thinking. Come on in and have a beer".

*

Ben cleared the patch rather well and dug a small foundation for the intended rocks. Will grudgingly took his spade and set to work when he had left, praying he would not return with Agnes as they had done when he was digging behind the altar. Luckily, only the neighbour's cat came to watch him and when it decided there was nothing to be gained walked away slowly, twitching its tail as though irritated that all this labour had not produced a field mouse or two. A robin was his next visitor but its attitude was quite different and seemed happy at every turn of his spade.

He wiped the sweat from his forehead as he drunk a glass of beer which Rosie had brought him.

"How deep do you want to go?", she asked, her voice sounding slightly tense.

"As far as I can before a pair of handcuffs are clicked on my wrists".

"You worry too much".

"So should you".

"Let me know when you're finished".

"Thanks for the support", he muttered, wondering how it was possible he was hiding his father's bones while one of the perpetrators of his death calmly read books on growing biological vegetables.

The gardeners came and, under the supervision of Arnie, laid a rockery along with a small stream of water which gently trickled down the Purbeck stones. He shuddered at the rising costs but his priority was to find Reggie a permanent home, bury him for eternity, so they could get on with their lives. Rosie thought they would meet up with him again in some parallel world.

"Heaven forbid", he had muttered, in horror, as he walked away quickly in case the discussion broadened.

Will could see Arnie and Rosie were in their element and followed each other around the rows of biological veggies. He smiled, Rosie was off his back and seemed to be extraordinarily happy. He could get on with his life which mostly consisted of patching up the house. Still, it could have been worse, he thought, so long as he could pay the bank every month then nothing was amiss.

*

It was the end of Spring when Poppy came to visit. She was surprised not only at the conservatory and fountain but at the rockery and the extensive planting of flowers and vegetables.

"You have made a lot of changes", she observed. "I wonder what Stella would think, she liked gardening. Sometimes, when the sun shone".

She watched her son that evening and thought she knew him well enough to recognised the signs of stress. She thought only a mother knew her child, even a prodigal mother. She guessed he had a financial problem so she thought it was time to step in and offer a solution which would not only benefit him but her as well.

"You do realise that I have some money put away. It's all yours", she informed him, a couple of days later. "You can have it now, if you like. I'm sure you can use it".

Will smiled but it was an uncertain smile.

"Think about it", she added, softly.

"Thanks Poppy, if I can just chew on it for a few days", he answered, aware that everything had a price tag.

Poppy was reading in the Conservatory that evening when a young woman and her mother came to the door. It appeared she was going to marry in September, a rather quick unexpected wedding, and had heard how beautiful their old chapel had become and how the garden was a sight to be seen.

Will raised his eyebrows as Rosie gushed enthusiasm and asked if she could help in any way.

"Well", said the mother, who called herself Pat. "We were wondering if we could use this beautiful room for the reception, perhaps even for the wedding seeing how it was once a chapel".

Rosie stepped back in amazement. "Well, yes, as far as I am concerned. But I don't have the facility to serve food. I mean I can't do the catering, not for a wedding".

Pat assured her that would be taken care of by an outside caterer who would only have to put their equipment in the kitchen and supply the tables and chairs.

"And the wedding, I don't know if you are allowed to marry here", she added, now sounding a bit breathless.

"Oh, my husband, George, will arrange for the Registrar to come here. He is so good at organising".

Rosie frowned, the names George and Pat rang a bell, someone had mentioned them. She would have to think about who it had been.

"Emy", she said, out loud, as though the name had been put in her mouth.

"Emy", repeated Pat, looking concerned.

"I believe you went on holiday with Emy and Jack Nielson".

Pat shifted uncomfortably. "We try to forget about it, strange couple", she added, her tone indicating the subject closed.

"She told me what happened", Rosie informed her, as though protecting Emy's good name.

"I heard she drowned recently in a lake", Pat said, suddenly open to any gossipy news.

"Yes, her friend tripped and fell against her and, somehow, she fell into the lake. She was rescued, of course, but later she died of secondary drowning".

"How tragic", Pat remarked, without showing any emotion. "She should have known better, she should have known to keep away from water after their holiday fiasco. Now let's get down to business".

It seemed to Will that all was signed and sealed within the hour and he glanced over to Poppy who seemed completely fascinated by the turn of events.

"Do you know", Poppy said, after they had left. "I have been thinking these last few days that, indeed, this could be used as some kind of a centre for events. I must say weddings had not come into my mind. If you were to divide the garden into little areas with tables and chairs and old objects from past gardens, pottery, urns, old gardening tools, wicker baskets and what have you, it would be really charming, really charming".

Will thought Rosie was about to explode with happiness.

"Marvellous idea", she gasped. "Arnie can make the plans and plant it out".

*

It only took a couple of good summers for 'Tower Lodge' to become known for its teas. Poppy helped with the scones and cakes, a Chef was hired for parties, Agnes helped in the kitchen and Ben helped in the garden when Arnie suffered a feminine breakdown, mostly when the Feng Shui plants took on a life of their own or after the rabbits feasted on his biological lettuces.

Slowly their red bank account changed to black. Poppy sold her flat by the sea and invested in 'Tower Lodge' by converting three rooms for herself; one a bedroom with an 'en suite' and the other a sitting room with a corner for making coffee or tea.

Later, she stripped Rosie's old comfortable kitchen and installed a new one, which would be the envy of any restaurateur. Then she modernised the whole house beginning with the central heating which she found above and beyond all other necessary requirements.

"You know", Poppy said one evening. "I was sitting in the garden when I saw a toad in the rockery. He had his head poking out from a space between the stones".

"It was probably a frog", Will answered, too quickly, suddenly overcome by something not quite natural.

"No it was a toad. He walked, he didn't jump, and he was brown with lots of ugly markings on him. I would know a toad anywhere".

"Well, so long as he feels at home", muttered Rosie, avoiding Will's glance.

Poppy laughed a little too loudly. "Do you know, I think I'll put a 'toad in the hole' on the menu for the children. They love sausages cooked in batter in the oven. Reggie was a toad", Poppy laughed again. "And most missing people are under the rockery", she added, grinning knowingly.

"Who knows", Will chuckled, trying to sound amused.

"Not me", Poppy answered, dunking her biscuit into her cup of coffee. "And if I did know, then it would go with me to my grave".

Rosie thought Will was about to have a fit for his face became slowly bright red and his hands trembled slightly as he placed his cup on the saucer.

Poppy put her hand in her pocket. "Look what I found this morning on top of that heap of sand in the corner of the garden".

"What?", answered Rosie.

"A bone. I think it's a phalange, a toe bone. I was a trainee nurse and we had to learn all the bones in the body. I've never forgotten, it was so stamped into us. I think your interest in archaeology came from me, Will".

"Could be from a rabbit", laughed Rosie a little stiffly. "Would you like another cup of coffee".

"Would you like something in it", Will asked, hoping that might silence his dried up old mother who had an equally dry humour.

"Not now", answered Poppy, smiling. "I think I'll make a 'Toad in the Hole', tomorrow. Then we'll drink to the other toad. God rest his soul".

*   *   *

HELEN

Helen BENNETT SWAM for as far as she could underwater. That idiot, Michael Lee, had accused her of killing Emy Nielson then threatened and humiliated her. No one did that.

He had come down to the cottage after Emy's Inquest, pointed a gun at her head, and forced her to row to the middle of the lake. Then he told her to jump in, either she did what he said or he would shoot her. She had jumped in, what else could she do. He was pointing the gun in the air when she surfaced.

"Helen", he had shouted, pulling the trigger several times, "it's not loaded".

Swimming back did not bothered her, she knew the lake like the back of her hand, she would survive and then he had better look out. If she hated someone enough she would make sure they eventually disappeared out of her life, out of everyone's life, if possible.

She was not far from the bank when she was overwhelmed by cramp in the back of her legs. She thrashed the water wildly from fear and desperation and looked back in the hope Michael Lee was near enough to help her, but it seemed he was too far away to hear her screams. She realised she would drown unless she concentrated on surviving and she struggled to turn her uncontrolled movements into a frantic dog paddle. 'I will win", she thought, as she heaved herself forward trying to focus on the years after Rob had died. The freedom his death had brought and the drastic events which followed.

She had tried to warn Rob that he had not skated for years and falling on his backside, at his age, would be just a painful exercise. He had not listened and that was his mistake.

The ice had cracked into razor sharp shards as he slowly sunk into the freezing water. A group of disbelieving skaters had looked on in horror, unable to help him, acutely aware of their own fragility as they carefully made their way to the bank of the lake.

Rob's mother, Belle, who was with them at the time, was worrying about her son being late. He was late, forever late, and Belle had run out into the early evening dark screaming for her son, her only child. Of course, she knew she should have gone after her, brought her back, warmed her, comforted her, but she had not done so. Nor did she report Belle missing to the police who were buzzing around half the night. Instead she mentioned it casually to Jack Nielson, Rob's best friend and her future lover, when he and his wife, Emy, arrived early the next morning. She had pretended to look shocked and devastated when they discovered Belle's body in the reeds and said that, most probably, the old lady had gone out in the middle of the night without her knowing. Everyone believed her, it was all so incredibly easy.

She had long concluded that the best laid plans seldom worked simply because people did the unexpected and that seizing a random opportunity was the one most likely to succeed.

Later, she had stood out on the mooring and wondered how she had suddenly lost two burdens in her life.

"Two birds with one stone", she had whispered, aware that she would inherit a small fortune. Surely, she thought, some benevolent spirit was looking after her, opening the door a little wider so that she could entice Jack into her life. Jack who she adored. Jack who had bought a motorbike so that he could race away in search of freedom while his homely little wife played the martyr. Though, in fairness, there was not a great deal Emy could do except perhaps check up on him. Had she done so she would, sooner or later, have found them together. Surely, Emy must have realised her lack of curiosity would have consequences.

*

It had been a beautiful summer's day when she lured Emy to the cottage. She had, surprisingly, accepted her invitation to collect Jack's tools which he had lent to Rob before he died.

She considered Emy to be naive, to say the least, and to some degree even deserved her fate since she was vaguely aware that going to the cottage alone could be unwise. But, true to form, Emy had trusted her. What did she think was going to happen, a cosy farewell while she apologised for seducing her husband which, incidentally, he more than enjoyed. Did she really think their last meeting together was going to be sisterly. 'We can still be friends. I promise not to see Jack again' scenario. Like hell. Not.

She had arranged, she thought quite cleverly, for Emy to fall off the mooring into the green water. She had jumped in after her followed by Daisy, Emy's wretched little poodle who reacted to her screams. She had eased her away from the old wooden piles, telling herself that she was not helping Emy to drown but rather not helping her to survive. Then, to her horror, she suddenly saw Jack pulling off his shoes and shirt as he launched himself forward into the lake and swim desperately towards his silly wife.

The timing could not have been worse and, of course, she had to change her plans and help to save the very person who she was trying not to save.

"I'll take her home", Jack puffed, now out of breath, as he supported Emy to the cottage.

"No, let her rest for a while. We have to take off her wet clothes, she can't go home like this. Help me to get her upstairs".

Emy was still coughing badly when they laid her on the bed. They washed her down and put on a T-shirt which read 'Sweet Dreams'.

Jack took Emy's hand and stroked her cheek.

"Try to rest for a few minutes. Would you like something, a drink or another pillow? It might help you to breathe easier", he asked, kindly.

She did not answer.

"I'm just going downstairs. I have to take these wet clothes off", he smiled. "I'll be back in a minute. Try to relax, darling".

He was in the lounge when Emy called again, he looked up the stairs and, for a moment, she had thought he might return but instead he walked into the garden. "I'll go up in a minute, I must first get out of these clothes".

"Come on, Jack", she had said, brightly. "I'll get you a towel".

He had wrapped the towel around his waist, covering the parts she loved so much, and hung his trousers and underpants in the sun to dry.

She had taken a quick shower, changed into a loose hanging dress with only a brief pair of panties underneath, and returned to the kitchen. Then she made a skimpy lunch washed down with generous glasses of red wine until she decided neither she nor Jack were fit to drive home.

Jack had been uneasy and insisted he looked in on his wife but she had persuaded him to stay with her by sitting astride his lap as he sat on a kitchen chair. He had tried to push her off and that had made her angry. No one had ever refused her except Rob who, in her opinion, had always been sexually dead. Now he was dead, physically dead.

Eventually, Jack had gone upstairs to see how Emy was recovering and, seconds later, she had heard the most terrible cry.

"Anything wrong?", she called.

Well, the rest was history. Jack had, also true to form, been unable to take even the most simple step such as calling for an ambulance and she was seriously irritated at his emotional crying and sobbing to the paramedics; how he had not realised how ill his wife was; how he thought she was sleeping.

It had not bothered her, it would be alright when the noise abated, when they had established their routine again. This time with a ring on her finger. Emy had a rather nice diamond ring. She thought she would take that, if one of her girls had not already slipped it onto an expectant finger.

However, it had not gone entirely to plan. Jack had blamed himself more than he did her and their love nest had been abandoned. He had promised to call her when Sophie and Jillie were more receptive to the idea. That was already months ago and every week which passed seemed like an eternity. She refused to accept he would end their affair, she could not accept he did not need her as she did him. Now she would have to woe him, connive, wriggle back into his life and he into her body.

She wondered whether she would have been different if her marriage to Rob had been normal;

whether she would have felt less hate and jealousy; schemed less; demanded less; not be prepared to go to extreme lengths to get what she wanted. She thought she would have been different and she wished she could be different. That was one of the reasons she had so disliked Emy, she did not have to be different.

✤

She was exhausted when she crawled up the muddy bank of the lake and made her way back to her cottage. There was no sign of Michael Lee or his car and for the first time she was afraid of the loneliness, the isolation, she had become so used to. She considered putting the cottage on the market. She could meet Jack somewhere else, in some other cosy nest. She gave a wishful sigh at the memory of her numerous ecstasies which seemed to her instantaneous for just his presence gave her joy.

She turned her thoughts back again to Michael Lee as she showered. He had warned her not to go to the police to report their differences and if she did he would tell them about she and Jack. She really did not know what Emy had told him, it seemed the two of them had some kind of special friendship but she was not sure how special it was. Possibly sexual but, on the other hand, she had always considered Emy to be rather straight laced, tight arsed would be the term used nowadays. Even so, she could not be entirely sure whether Michael Lee knew enough to make the police suspicious of Emy's death. She thought it was not worth the risk.

She would have to think of some way to pay him back, to wipe the supercilious grin off his face. She would have to give it some thought.

She closed her eyes and let the hot shower beat down on her as she imagined Jack stood close behind her, his hands caressing her body while he kissed her neck.

She drove home that evening, too insecure to stay in the cottage alone, at least for a while. She thought of Rob, something she tried not to do too often, and how they had met.

Her father had been sent to work in Singapore and she, without a steady boyfriend or a particularly interesting career, had accompanied her parents and joined the club. The club of young women who were looking for husbands, successful young men who could offer them a good life both out east and at home in Europe. Rob had ticked all the boxes, he was handsome, overseas manager of a company which imported luxury goods, earned a good salary with an excellent bonus every year, pension scheme and above average home leave. It was her mother who had pointed out Rob's financial advantages which had not been the reason for her enthusiasm, but rather she had revelled in making her girlfriends jealous by having such a handsome beau.

They had married quite quickly, actually within four months, which had surprised her and her parents, who seemed uneasy at the speed of their courtship. Her mother had openly asked her if she was pregnant and her father even seemed to have some kind of aversion to Rob himself.

Rob's parents had come over for the wedding. His mother, Belle, a narrow minded woman, did not seem in favour of either her or the idea of Rob getting married. His father, Charles, was different. He was an extrovert, humorous, witty, but critical of his son though she did not know why.

The sun was low now and she turned her headlights on. "Almost dark", she murmured, returning to her marriage. "My wedding night", she grimaced as she spoke.

She had been a virgin and had no way of judging how love should be. Looking back, she realised how quick, rushed, the first time had been as though it was something to get out of the way. She had been disappointed for she had imagined it would be something special, a something which would carry her into a realm of yet unknown delights. Instead, it had been painful and messy and not really a something she would want to remember or even do again though, of course, there was always the possibility of being overtaken by a storm of passion, thunder and lightning. Instead, their spasmodic lovemaking remained a soft drizzle.

It had not taken long for her to realise she had been trapped for Rob needed to cover up his sexual inadequacy to the world at large. Marriage would keep women at bay and even men who found his fine features, blond hair and slight build attractive. She was young and inexperienced and had become seriously unsure and insecure.

Rob's mother, and even her own mother, had hinted about her supplying an offspring. She had wanted to shout, 'Ask Rob. Ask him why he can't get it up. It's not me, it's him'. But she ignored them, kept her pride, said nothing, and gave up any hope of having a normal married life. She was caught in an almost sexless marriage with a man who showed no inclination to alter the situation. She had resigned herself to a life of useless coffee parties and afternoons at the swimming pool with spoilt, grizzling, children who were too young, hot and sticky, to appreciate their mothers' lifestyle.

She had despaired for the choice was either to accept it, or not.

The only person who seemed to guess there was a problem was Rob's best friend, Jack, who she found excruciatingly handsome. She had tried to get him on her side, into her bed, but he had remained loyal to his best friend, which she had found disappointing since he was the 'not' she was desperately seeking.

Then Jack had an open affair with a beautiful Chinese girl, called Jade, who had just broken up with her boyfriend. Jade had held a party and Jack had stayed the night, in fact many nights. He admitted to Rob that he had been careless. Rob was sympathetic and she was scathing. Then, to everyone's relief Jade dropped Jack for another lover, at least he thought there was someone else, though he did not know who it was. Anyway, he had been happy to be let off the proverbial 'hook' and so was she.

She had been heartbroken when Jack was called back to London. Once in a while he and Rob met up for a drink, when they returned on home leave, to which she was never invited. The depth of her jealousy surprised her when she heard Jack had married Emy, a divorcee with a daughter called Sophie, and who later had another daughter with Jack, Jillie. Most probably Jillian. She sneered as she sung the nursery rhyme, 'Jack and Jill went up the hill'.

She decided this 'Emy woman' to be rather simple and that it would not be difficult to usurp her. Conquer Jack by whatever means necessary. She thought that possible, once 'the icing was off the matrimonial cake'.

Of course, she had a few flings in Singapore but none of them had come to anything and years later, back in the U.K., it seemed even more difficult finding someone who was not already bagged. The average wife seemed possessive, suspicious, vigilant and she assumed checked their husbands on a regular basis. She almost felt sorry for these men in bondage.

Only Rob's father, Charles, was free to do what he wanted for Belle gave him a remarkably long line. 'The longer the lead the further they go', she muttered. She smiled as she remembered how, when they returned on home leave, Belle claimed Rob and went off for hours leaving she and Charles to amuse themselves. After some weeks, and afternoons of flirting, the obvious happened.

"We're alone again", Charles had grinned.

"What shall we do?", she asked, responding to the suggestive glint in his eyes, as she fell back onto the sofa with her legs slightly apart and her arm raised on a cushion.

He sat next to her and she fingered the buttons on his shirt. He kissed her hand, then bent over her. She welcomed his kisses, hot, desperate, kisses known by those who received too little passion, who needed to be loved and to return love.

"Oh, Helen", he whispered. "Sine amor, nihil est vita".

"What's that?", she asked, softly.

"Without love, life is pointless", he answered. "I teach the little morons Latin", he added, now half lying on top of her. "Life is nothing without love", he groaned.

She loosened her blouse and he felt for her breasts. He smiled and she knew what he was thinking.

"Klein maar fijn", she whispered.

He stopped. "What does that mean?".

"I had a Dutch boyfriend, long before I knew Rob", she lied. "It means, small but fine".

He smiled at her gently. "I'm not greedy, they're enough for me. Amor est caecus".

"And?".
"Love is blind", he murmured.
"I hope your sight doesn't improve".
"Klein maar fijn. I'll remember that".
And he did, whenever they met he whispered those words as he greeted her.

Years later, she laid red roses on his grave. The card read, 'Sine amor, nihil est vita'.

*   *   *

MICHAEL LEE

IT WAS ALMOST DARK WHEN Michael Lee eventually arrived at Monty's house to return the gun after yesterday's scene at the lake. He sat in his sports car for a few minutes remembering the day his mother, Jade, had told him they were going to the U.K.

＊

He had been looking in the newspaper for a job, or even an inexpensive IT course, when his mother pulled the newspaper down, peered over the top, and told him not to bother to look.

He had looked up, irritated she had interrupted his search.

"We are going on holiday", she informed him, smiling broadly.

"On holiday, where on holiday?", he repeated, sounding surprised.

"Britain, England".

"England. Where in England?".

"The south coast. To Monty. He has invited us to stay for a month".

"How come?".

"He found us, we found each other".

He had known about Monty, his mother had talked with great fondness about him. How he had stood by her when life was difficult but, after a disagreement in his office, he had returned to the U.K. He had been offered a good job in London which he could not refuse. He had left and they had lost touch.

"When are we going?".

"The moment your exam results are known".

"And a job then, everyone else will have found something before I get back".

"We'll cross that bridge when we come to it".

Monty had met them at the airport and driven straight down to Devon. His mother had acted coyly, flirtatiously, as though she was on a first date. A few weeks later, they announced they were to marry. He could hardly believe it. He could understand his mother would have a good life, would no longer have to work, but the idea of leaving a bustling city, like Singapore, for the extreme quiet of a small village by the sea, in Devon, was not what he was looking for. Not at seventeen, without his peers.

He had not been happy at the prospect of living in the back of beyond, no matter what its beauty. Monty had understood his misgivings and offered to find a college in or around London.

"You see, you'll settle down. Just give it time".

He hadn't been so sure about that, he wasn't going to make any promises though he had realised he was tied down, eight thousand miles away from home and without any money. He had felt frustrated for he had been trying to find his father, Jimmy Lee, a missing parent who shared a common surname with his mother. She had told him many times when he was a small boy how his father had let her down. It was only when he grew older did he realise what she meant. The old story, girl loves man, man is married. Nothing new about that, he had thought.

He had tried to question her but she had remained secretive.

"Not now", she would snap, dismissively, gesturing with her hand whenever he broached the subject.

"It's not over yet, Mum. I'll find him with or without your help".

Amazingly, Monty turned out to be all his mother had said. He bought a beach house which he and his eventual friends could use weekends and holidays. Of course, it was a 'win-win' situation, he happy while the romantic couple enjoyed their privacy.

Then, some years ago, he had arranged to

meet his mother there. He was excited, he had saved enough money for a return ticket home, an old school friend had offered to put him up and he had a lead on his father.

Their meeting had gone disastrously wrong. It had been a wild, stormy, Sunday afternoon and his mother obviously did not want him to come down from London. But he had done so, he was enthusiastic and wanted to share his news.

It was on that fateful afternoon when his mother admitted Jimmy Lee was not his father and was even unsure who was. He was stunned, breathless, wordless and then angry, enraged at her deceit and lies. Years of deceit and lies.

He had bullied her, screamed at her, called her names, until she had eventually walked out onto the patio and slowly down to the shoreline. He had watched her standing in the fierce wind with the rain beating down on her and he had felt even more angry that she had not stayed to finish the fight. He needed to hear her cry, see her grovel for his forgiveness. He had run after her and pushed her, again and again, until she finally lost her balance and fell backwards into the bitterly cold water. She had pulled herself up, her jacket open, her wet clothes sticking to her shivering body, her hair flat against her head. She had stared at him, tearfully, unable to comprehend his anger and hate.

"You're a slut, anyone's lay. You don't even know who my father is".

"What difference does it make. I love you", she cried, her voice barely audible in the wind.

Of course, he felt guilty but somewhere, deep down, he thought his mother had behaved badly and bad things happen to people who do bad things. At least, that is what she had always taught him and it seemed she was right.

He did not want to think about it, he did not want to relive that afternoon. It did no good to playback what happened. He had learnt to let it go, see it as a part of life. Not a good part but, nevertheless, a part.

He had shelved the idea of looking for Jimmy Lee for he felt an obligation to stay with Monty for a while. He could not just leave him in what seemed to be deep mourning, grieving for his mother. But he had been wrong about that for Sophie, who was about his age, arrived in Monty's life. It had surprised him though he realised his stepfather was vulnerable to the charms of such a young woman.

He thought he would stay around until he was sure Monty and Sophie were an 'item'. He was, in fact, on the point of renewing his plans to look for his father when suddenly Monty died of a heart attack. He could not believe it. Monty had seemed so relaxed, he was even planning to marry Sophie.

The only good which came out of all the unhappiness was his independence. Except for a small amount of money which Monty left Sophie, he had inherited all of his estate.

Sophie, who was now free, had been on his wish list from the moment they met. He thought he would take his time, sympathise and eventually win her over. He mostly got what he wanted.

And Sophie's mother? Well, she was to be considered. He had met her at the beach house with Sophie. He and Emily Nielson had clicked, perhaps she felt motherly towards him, perhaps he felt sexual towards her. Whichever one it was, he had offered her the use of the beach house until the following summer, or even longer. He thought they could meet up. Anything could happen in such a setting. Two on his wish list, mother and daughter, that would be a 'first'. A super conquest.

He had flown to Singapore a few days later and found the man who was not his father.

Jimmy Lee had told him the truth about his love for his mother, Jade, and how circumstances ended their affair. He had even recently suggested he should return to his land of birth and he would find him a very good position in his company, even though he was semi-retired.

He had returned to settle Monty's estate, to sell the house and auction off the valuable items. It had taken some time, partly due to the local solicitor who worked at a snail's pace and seemed unaware of the modern world around him. Of course, Sophie had rummaged through everything before it was taken to the charity shop or simply thrown away.

He had left the attic until last and remembered his surprise at finding a large metal box containing a police uniform and papers, all dating back to when Monty's father was in the Hong Kong police force. He had sat back amazed as he pulled out a gun and a box of bullets. He had checked the gun was not loaded and taken it home.

❖

He frowned as he fingered the gun in his pocket, remembering how he had attended Emy's Inquest the day before and how he had watched Helen swimming strongly towards the bank until suddenly he heard her shouting for help. He had rowed on and only once turned around to see her thrashing wildly in the water. He thought Emy must have done that, now Helen would know how it felt. He had no regrets, she deserved what she got. Sooner or later he would hear whether she was dead, alive or missing.

The house was cold and too silent when he eventually entered the hall and climbed the stairs to the shadowy attic. He quickly put the light on so that he could recognised the spooky forms and shivered as he once again opened the chest and slipped the gun, clean of fingerprints, between the policeman's uniform. Should Helen report him to the police he could always deny her story. What gun! He would take the chest home when the house was sold.

He was about to pull the lid down when he saw a small wooden box covered by an old felt hat.

He took it out, closed the chest and hurried back downstairs to his bedroom locking the attic door behind him as though someone, something, might follow him.

He sat on his bed and glanced around at all the familiar items which had seemed important to him in his youth, possessions he now viewed as sentimental rubbish. He nervously opened the box to find a bundle of letters to and from Monty and his mother reminiscing old times. Finally, a letter from Monty inviting them for a holiday and another asking his mother for her bank account number so that he could deposit money for their fares. She was not to worry, he would take care them.

"You knew we were going to stay here before we left. You knew we were not going back to Singapore. More lies, mother, more lies", he shouted.

His anger mounted as he viewed his mother with contempt. A woman who had affairs, perhaps simultaneously and obviously carelessly, and did not know who his father was.

He threw a book across the room in frustration, it hit a photograph of his mother. The glass broke as it hit the floor. He thought that was an omen, only he did not know if was a good or a bad one.

He was just going back downstairs when he noticed the silhouette of a man in the entrance of the now open front door. Fear ran through him for he was not heavily built and knew he could never win if attacked.

"What do you want?", he asked, sharply.

"Hello, Mike. I saw you arrive".

"Mr. Harris, you gave me a shock", he sighed with relief. "I haven't seen you for some time".

"Sorry if I startled you. I saw your car outside. I just wanted to ask you how things are going".

"Very well, thank you. I wanted to tell you that I've managed to find a home for Monty's birds including the peacock. They're going to a nice estate in Hampshire. And I've arranged for the gardener to carry on feeding them and to clean the cages", he informed Monty's old neighbour.

"That's good news. I've been meaning to speak with you. You know, I missed Monty's funeral because I was at home with another asthma attack".

"Yes, I know. It's alright, don't worry about it".

"I saw the ambulance arrive just after a lady left his house", he added, guessing this bit of information might be possible food for thought.

"What lady? I didn't know anyone was with Monty when he died".

"Oh, but there was. She arrived at the house just a minute before Monty and then left just before the ambulance arrived".

"You say she left before the ambulance came".

"Yes, that's right. I wasn't dressed and I only saw what happened because I was standing by my bedroom window. As I said, she arrived just before Monty. She seemed angry. I could hear her shout at him. The window was open", he explained, looking slightly uncomfortable. "I didn't report it because two days later it was in the local newspaper. If his death had been suspicious then I would have said something".

"Thanks for telling me, Mr. Harris. I think I know who it was. I guess Monty called for an ambulance himself. They can be very quick especially if they're in the area".

"That's what I thought, they must have been in the village when the call came through". His tone suggested disbelief at his own theory.

"That must have been it. Do you still need the key to the house?".

"No, take it back, Mike. The estate agent has one now".

"Thanks again", he said, kindly, taking the key as he opened the front door wider. "I'll be here when they come for the birds. There is someone interested in buying the house", he added, thinking he owed the old man just a little information.

He walked thoughtfully to the kitchen, convinced the mystery woman must have been Emy. He recollected Monty telling him how she was going to stay a couple of nights in the village so that he could tell her about his affair with Sophie and how they intended to marry. Emy had gone alone, without Jack, less than a week before Monty died. Why then would she return so quickly and, surely, if Monty had been taken ill while she was with him she would have waited for the ambulance.

He felt overwhelmed with the idea that Sophie might know more than she was telling and he wondered what Jack knew, probably nothing seeing how he had treated his home as a doss house, bed and breakfast, catch up with the post and move on. Coming and going as it suited him.

Emy had told him that and also how Jack was seeing Helen Bennett but, actually, she did not want to know whether they were having an affair. He thought she was unusual since most women were like hunters, stalking their prey, their husbands, their lovers. Unable to accept blissful ignorance as she had done. He was unsure whether he should admire her resilience to the truth, or not.

He turned his thoughts back to Sophie. He had already tried to date her but she said she still missed Monty and wanted to build her career.

That had irritated him, he did not like being put 'on hold' or rejected. He knew he looked friendly, due to his grin and laid back appearance, but he was not as easy going as people thought. In fact, he considered himself to be quite complicated and not someone to be pushed around.

He thought he could coax Sophie with a good dinner and expensive wine, followed by a drink at his place. She was impressed by his new apartment near the West End, he had watched her carefully as she walked around. He knew she would like to have a place like his, maybe a slightly larger pad since she had a child. Sophie could not be allowed to escape so easily, he would get her in the end, amuse her for a while and then he would consider Jimmy Lee's offer to work for his company in Singapore.

*

The peacock woke him up and he laid reminiscing the old days when his mother fussed around him. She was actually a good mother and even a good wife but there was always something between she and Monty. Something he could not place.

He had shown Emy a photograph of a Chinese New Year's party held by his mother when she was young, before he was born. She was surrounded by her friends including Rob, Helen, Monty and Jack. Later, Emy had become obsessed with finding his father, after hearing that it was not Jimmy Lee, and began a search for the truth starting with Jack and Monty. It seemed the New Year's party had freed his mother's inhibitions.

Gradually, he had found himself the centre of Emy's universe and enjoyed her excessive interest in him. He had never been so important to a woman before, not even his mother had lavished so much attention on him. He even wondered whether his passing interest in Sophie might have something to do with her mother, the forbidden was so much more exciting than the available. He was uncertain of his agenda, whether to 'love and to hold' Sophie, or 'to love and discard' her.

Monty had turned out to be the culprit, if one could call him that, with Jack as the runner-up. They were the two who had enjoyed his mother's favours, simultaneously enjoyed them. He was undecided about his feelings towards his mother, was she the loose woman he had accused her of being or was she just a sad looser, manipulated by opportunists.

For the first time he felt sympathetic towards his mother and wished now he had given her a chance to explain what had happened in her difficult youth. He thought of Jack again. Jack the Peter Pan who had raced around on his motorbike while Emy waited for him at home. Jack a poodle, a wimp under Helen's control. Jack who had screwed his mother when she was young and vulnerable. Helen the viper, the snake in the grass, his loyal lover.

He drove reluctantly to the beach house, something he had not done for a long time. He clenched his jaw as he made his way down to the shoreline where his mother had thrown herself into the crashing surf. He had told himself that she did not have to do that, it was her choice, an unnecessary tragedy. Later, it appeared she was aware of her terminal illness and he thought it likely that his uncontrolled anger had precipitated her final decision. He could not condone his behaviour but, at least, her action had a purpose, one which helped him to suppress his guilt. He was proud of her for being so brave, so decisive, though he wished she had stayed to finish the fight. He was sure that, eventually, he would have forgiven her and made it up, even helped her when she became seriously ill.

He dismissed his unwanted thoughts as he climbed back up the sand dunes to the desolate house and flopped into an arm chair, the one which Emy had sat in while he knelt next to her on the floor and told her how he had taken risks to cover up his mother's suicide. How he would have been in terrible trouble if anyone had seen him; if the authorities could prove he had lied.

At first, Emy had been angry but he had managed to regain her sympathy. She had stroked his hair and he had lifted his head up to her and, somehow, their lips had touched. He had slowly moved up her body until he was lying over her, kissing her breasts and running his hand down her body. She had shivered then, unwillingly, pushed him away. He had almost succeeded, he had been a wisp away from ticking one of the names on his wish list. He felt roused when he thought of it.

It was gone ten thirty when he looked at his watch, time to have a coffee in 'The Cutter', a small local inn with a few bedrooms used mostly by casual visitors rather than actual holiday makers. It was a popular little place decorated with seafaring objects together with large sea shells and unusual pieces of timber found on the beach. It had a charm, if you were looking for a nautical atmosphere.

He speeded along the winding lanes towards the outskirts of the village feeling unusually guilty, even regretful, at the idea of checking up on Emy. However, he convinced himself that she had not told him of her visit to Monty on the day he died. He was disappointed at her secrecy which helped him to dismiss his guilt.

He stepped over the well worn doorstep into the reception area where he planned to get a glance at the hotel register to see if Emy had stayed there.

He could immediately see the visitors' book on the desk. He glanced around, picked it up, hid it under his jacket and made his way to the toilet.

He could see Emy had booked in for two nights when she visited Monty but not on any of the days around his death. He hid the book under his jacket, as before, sauntered back to the reception area and placed it back on the desk as he made his way to the busy restaurant.

He was drinking a Cappuccino while he recalled how he had driven down from London to identify his stepfather. It had been a terrible experience and he had cried on the way back to Monty's house, hardly able to absorb the full meaning of his death for he was the only person he had left to fall back on.

Sophie had come and tearfully packed her possessions into boxes. She had hung onto him crying and he had rubbed her back and made her tea and said all the right things. They had kissed goodbye and promised to keep in touch. It had been a traumatic period and he reckoned she would need comforting, something he was very prepared to do, an act of kindness.

He had spent the following weeks and months emptying all the cupboards and drawers and leaving the 'en suite' bathrooms spotlessly clean. Only his own bedroom was left untouched, it was his sanctuary, a place to stay if he wanted.

Monty's cleaning lady had offered to help but he had refused. He did not want anyone snooping around, watching him, advising him.

He stopped, as though his thoughts literally froze, as though his mind slammed on a brake, as he remembered one of the spare bedrooms.

He could see the room in his thoughts, two windows on either side of the dressing table, built-in closets, a chest of drawers, two bedside tables and a bed. A queen-size bed with two duvets. Both had been turned down when he had stripped the covers off them and laid a bedspread across the mattress.

He stared at his now empty coffee cup as it dawned on him that the spare bedrooms were seldom used, if ever. Someone had slept in that bed, perhaps not 'one someone' but 'two someone's'. It had to be Emy, she was the last to visit. He could imagine Monty might have drunk too much and she had stayed the night. Knowing Monty's appreciation of good wine, he thought that was more than likely.

Of course, it was possible Emy had automatically turned down both duvets. He could hardly bring himself to accept that Emy had shared the bed with Monty while he was planning to tell her about his impending marriage to her daughter.

Now, he felt even more cheated that Emy had not told him any details about the two days she spent with him and, even worse, that she had been with him on the day he died. He felt puzzled at his sense of disappointment, rather like a child whispering a secret in the playground and receiving nothing in return.

"Bizarre", he muttered, aware he had also thought of both Sophie and Emy as future trophies. He wondered if it was possible that Monty had the same kinky thoughts. 'Like father, like son', he muttered, smiling broadly as he stood up to pay the bill.

Sophie agreed she would meet him the following Saturday so long as Peter would take Tom. He had recently become obsessed with the idea of saving Sophie and her offspring, just like Monty had saved him and his mother, but now it occurred to him that he was already seventeen when he arrived in England and Monty had not been obliged to raise him, suffer toys and rubbish, messy eating, spilt chocolate milk, scratches on his shiny furniture and all the rest of it.

He shuddered at the thought of his minimalistic apartment being less than that, his highly polished floor, his white transparent curtains, his perfect kitchen, his bathroom with towels hanging exactly in line with each other, all at the mercy of a small boy. His life was orderly and he did not think he was able, or wanted, to change it. He realised how Monty must have thought and that he had probably inherited his fear of sticky fingered and snotty nosed children from him. He shuddered again. He wanted Sophie but not her baggage, not some child from another marriage, not the hassle of an irritated father who was only interested in laying his latest girl friend and paying the minimum alimentation for his increasingly expensive offspring.

He did not want another man's child and all the complications which went with it. He wanted his own child who would not have to share love and possessions with another sibling from another marriage. Actually, he did not even know if Sophie wanted another child, maybe her career was the most important thing in her life.

He decided to continue his original plan, a romantic dinner, followed by a nightcap at his apartment and the ensuing night of love. Then he would drop her. He thought that would probably be the best for him, for her and her child.

Sophie looked tired on Saturday evening. She said she had worked late all week and was now paying someone to look after Tom during school holidays. She could leave him with Jack, when either she or her 'ex' could not look after him, but he was reluctant to have him for more than a couple of days at a time. He had said he was trying to get his life together and did not want to look after children for too long. She had felt hurt and wanted to shout at him that he would do it for Jillie, if and when the occasion arose, but not for her. She wasn't his child and Jillie was. That made the difference.

He felt stunned, Sophie was saying just what he had been thinking. It was as though she was confirming his thoughts.

He agreed with her, told her how he understood her feelings. Poured another glass of wine and commiserated. After all, he had also been a stepchild. He knew all about it.

"I never thought of it like that, Monty spoke so kindly of you. It never occurred to me he ever saw you as anything else but his son and in the end you were his child. What a pity he never knew it".

"My mother, Monty and Jack were all connected. Can you imagine a scandal, from over thirty years ago, coming back to haunt you?".

"What do you mean?".

"You don't know?".

"Know what?".

"Jack could have been my father. It was a tossup between him and Monty. It seems Monty was the alpha male".

Sophie stared across the table in amazement.

"Who told you that?"

"Your mother, she said Helen told her".

"You mean Jack had an affair with your mother, Jade, all those years ago and Helen told her about it. What was the point of doing that, unless it was to hurt her. Poor mum".

"Yes, Helen was a bitch to tell her. Monty told me he knew your mother and father in Singapore. What's his name? ", he added.

"Guy. Yes, he and my father worked in the same office".

"Did they socialise?".

"Hardly, they hated each other at that time, as far as I know".

"But not anymore?".

"No, they even looked each other up. Monty heard Guy was looking for a job for me. He knew of an opening and told Guy. Small world".

"But your mother didn't know that?".

"No, not until I told her".

"She must have felt uncomfortable with Monty and her 'ex' contacting each other behind her back. It all sounds a bit deceitful, poor Emy".

"Yes, I know, but I didn't expect it to end with Monty's death and then mum's. It all went so pear shaped. I can't begin to tell you how guilty I feel".

"Why should you feel guilty, you weren't responsible for their deaths. If anyone is guilty then it's Helen and Jack. It was their fault your mother died. I hate deceit", he added, staring across the room as he thought of what Mr. Harris had told him. "Did Monty ask your mother to visit him so that he could tell her about the two of you getting married?", he continued.

"Yes".

"And did he?".

"No, he got cold feet and left it to me. I went down to see him, he had "The Gull" in the water and we went sailing. I dropped in to tell mum on the way back Sunday evening. She was pretty angry about it all, she found him too old. She reacted really badly, I knew she would but in the end she seemed to accept it. But, knowing my mother, that doesn't say anything. That's why I asked Monty to tell her when I wasn't around".

"And did she confront Monty after you had told her".

"I don't know. It was all so quick. I suppose she could have 'phoned him".

"Monty died the following Thursday only a few days later".

"Yes", Sophie replied frowning. "Am I supposed to make some kind of a sum from that. Are you suggesting something?".

"No, but she could have gone down to see him, maybe they had a fight and he dropped dead".

"Oh come on. I don't believe that and you don't know that".

"No, I don't know that, just throwing a few scenario's around".

"Well don't", she snapped, sounding upset.

"It really doesn't matter. It doesn't change anything".

"I am wondering if you're right", she muttered, thoughtfully. "Maybe she did upset him and he had a heart attack".

"Try not to think about it", he said, kindly. "It doesn't help to chew over things you can't prove".

He stared at the menu card now certain Emy had visited Monty, probably had a fight with him and he had a heart attack. She must have 'phoned the ambulance and left quickly before it arrived, frightened of Sophie finding out she had been there. Sophie would never have forgiven her. He was pretty sure about that

He decided he would not say anything more for the time being. First things first, he thought. Upsetting her further would not help his cause.

He placed his hand over hers after the coffee had been served.

"Shall we go to my place for a nightcap?", he

suggested, leaning intimately towards her.

"Why not", replied Sophie, thinking of Mike's inheritance and the easy life it offered her. "By the way, you can't guess who 'phoned me the other day".

"Who?".

"The bitch, Helen"

"Is she still alive", he joked. "What did she want?".

"I don't really know except to tell me she is selling the cottage, as if I care. Oh, yes, she went on to ask me your address. I told her I couldn't give her that before asking you, but in the end I gave her your telephone number. I would have hung up if I had known all of this".

"It's okay. I don't mind speaking to her. Maybe she has something interesting to say", he answered, amused that Helen wanted to contact him since it was either a sign of weakness or that she was planning something devious to repay him for his dangerous intention at the lake. "Come on, let's go", he said, standing up and taking her chair.

"You have such nice manners, just like Monty", she remarked, partly because it was true and partly because she thought it might be time to take his interest in her seriously.

*

She had not planned to go to bed with Mike but the wine had got to her and she wanted to be loved and make love. By the time they arrived at his apartment she felt the beginning of a bad headache, probably from the wine, and decided to take a shower in the hope it might lessen.

She felt guilty as she undressed. She had locked the bathroom door so Mike could not join her. She still felt some loyalty towards Monty though she had come to realise that their age gap had been too much, both physically and mentally. She remembered the numerous times she had left Tom with his father when she went down to Devon. In fact, Monty hardly ever saw her offspring. He had hinted that he had looked after Jade's son and perhaps that was enough. She had wanted to say that Mike was hardly a child when he arrived, but she said nothing since it would have driven a wedge between them. Once he had even said, 'give him to Peter', as though he was a dispensable pet.

She had begun to accept that, most probably, her mother had been right. Monty's life style had paved the path of love. She tried to clear her thoughts, her memories of Monty, and consider whether it was wise to get involved with Mike.

She stood with her hands against the white tiles and let the hot water beat down on her neck and shoulders. She felt strangely overwhelmed by a sensation that there was something she should know, something she had forgotten, something in the past which she should recall. She thought again of her mother and felt as though she was her, that her mother had stood under a shower as she did now but she could not recall when, or where, that could have been. She felt herself overcome by a feeling that she must leave, not after sex with Mike, but now. She felt a panic which she had never experienced before, an urgency to get dressed and get out before reaching the point of no return. Get away from the past, Monty and now Michael Lee.

She dressed quickly and 'phoned Peter on her mobile.

"Can you pick me up?", she half whispered.

There was a pause. "Where are you?".

"At Mike Lee's place. I want to leave but I don't have my car and I don't want him to drive me home. You know where he lives?".

"Yes, you once told me".

"Well, there's a little Chinese restaurant opposite his flat. I'll be there in half an hour".

"Be careful. I don't like you walking over streets late at night. Wait downstairs in the lobby. I'll pick you up there".

"Okay, don't be too long".

She unlocked the bathroom door to find Mike standing behind it, obviously aware something was wrong. He looked at the mobile in her hand.

"Who are you calling?"

"Peter, I've asked him to pick me up. I don't feel well and you have drunk too much to drive".

He looked at her coldly. "You could have stayed here".

"I've arranged it. It's okay".

"Please yourself", he answered, coldly, as he

walked into the colourless lounge and played a cd.

He hardly turned his head when she opened the front door.

"Sorry, Mike", she murmured.

"I couldn't care less", he said, bitterly, as he turned the music up higher. "Oh, by the way", he added. "Your mother was with Monty when he died. She was probably the cause of his death".

"Liar", she screamed, hysterically.

"I can prove it, if you want me to. And I believe they slept together when she went down there those two days. No wonder he dropped dead when she returned a second time. She couldn't get enough of it, if you ask me".

Sophie stood shaking with anger and hurt.

"You pathetic liar, you disgusting nerd. I hope you drop dead. I hope", she screamed, hardly able to catch her breath, "I hope you smash your bloody sports car with you in it".

"And don't use my beach house again. I'm having the lock changed".

"Get lost. Do what you want. I hope I never see you again".

He called her a name under his breath when he later found the bathroom untidy and decided there was nothing deader than dead love. He had not meant to hurt her but she had rebuffed him and no one did that twice. There were plenty of others who would enjoy a night with him. Sophie had overstepped the mark, she had not even given him a chance to entice her, excite her. "The truth will out", he muttered. "Serves her right".

He fell back into his white armchair and thought of how his mother had worked long hours for various families while he sat in the kitchen doing his homework and, more often than not, helping to prepare vegetables or do other menial chores. He had seen how she had scrimped and saved for tickets to go to the U.K., at least up until Monty had sent her a big fat cheque, so to speak.

It seemed she was eternally grateful and showed it by pampering him and keeping his perfect house perfect and her willingness to please him sexually. At least, that was what he supposed since, once in a while, he listened outside their bedroom door. It was something he was not particularly proud of but he had a need to know.

He thought of Mia, Jimmy's granddaughter who he had met on his mission for truth. She was beautiful, fine, charming, well mannered. In fact, she became even more attractive with every passing day. He thought the time was nearing to visit Jimmy again and see what he had to offer and whether he could charm Mia out of the trees. He thought he could and, if not, then another.

*

Eventually, Helen telephoned. He was amazed at her friendliness and asked her directly what was the name of her game. She had laughed and said she was sorry that he felt she had purposely let Emy die. How could she know anything about secondary drowning. She was alright when she and Jack left her in bed. It had been a terrible tragedy and she hoped he would see it that way. Perhaps they could meet and have a drink together. She would try to convince him that she had been lonely after Rob had died and had known Jack way back in Singapore when he and Rob were still bachelors. Perhaps, she could persuade him to see her in a different light. She could tell him about the old days when everyone knew his mother as a beautiful young woman, hardly more than a girl, and desperately in love with Jimmy.

He had apologised for his behaviour at the lake. He said he had watched her swimming, he would never have let her drown.

She silently mouthed "Liar" as he talked on.

It seemed to him that she accepted his apology and they agreed to meet at a small Bistro near Hampstead Heath. She would book the table.

He snapped his mobile closed and laid back, enjoying the various scenario's which might take place. He liked older women, unprotected sex, no surprise pregnancies. Their characters formed, no need to grow towards each other, the give and take costing years only to realise that one of them always took more than the other. He thought mostly the woman wanted to change the man, first get married and then to work.

"The Changlings", he muttered, to himself. No, he definitely did not fall into that category. If anyone had to change it would be the woman, she the weaker sex, subservient, would have to please him. He didn't think he needed to change the status quo by adapting to some woman's idea of Mr. Perfect.

Yes, he thought, he might string Helen along for a while. He thought they might find some common ground, even if it was only their intense dislike of each other.

*   *   *

Ann Bailey

SOPHIE and PETER

It WAS THE FIRST TIME SOPHIE had driven alone with Peter for what seemed ages. She could remember how she had fallen in love with him at college and how they motored around in his old Fiat Panda which was, rather like its place of origin, temperamental.

They had lived together for some years after leaving college. She had become pregnant and expected Peter to tell her to get an abortion but, perhaps because of his upbringing, he insisted they should marry. She had been elated, to marry your first love was almost unthinkable. All had gone well for some years, in fact their actual marriage had lasted five years which she later heard was the average for a 'first time around'.

"How is Salome?", she asked, before they got to his flat.

"I've told you her name is Sallyann".

"I always get it wrong".

"You get a lot wrong".
"For example?".
He did not answer.

The flat was warm and cosy, Sallyann was in Peter's dressing gown stirring a cup of hot chocolate and did not hide her surprise when Sophie entered.

"I thought Sophie could share Tom's bed".

Sallyann did not react to his statement.

"No, that's okay. I'll pick up Tom now, if you'll take us home. Leave you two in peace", Sophie suggested, to break the atmosphere.

"No, it's too late", replied Peter, firmly.

"If she stays, I'm going", snapped Sallyann, angrily.

"Do what you want, it's up to you".

"I can go, no problem", Sophie repeated, not wanting to be in the middle of a fight.

Peter did not answer.

"Fine, I'm off. Luckily, I have my own car, I don't have to rely on my ex-husband to look after me", Sallyann announced as she walked into the bedroom and slammed the door.

"I had no intention of making a scene", she said, guiltily.

"It's okay. Don't worry about it".

"This is what you want, isn't it?".

"To be honest, yes".

"Am I being used?", she asked, wearily.

"No. We have to talk".

"What about?".

"Us".

"Us", she repeated.

Sallyann came out of the bedroom with a large bag hanging over her shoulder. She gave her now ex-boyfriend a hard look.

"Good luck with the bitch", she shouted, banging out of the front door.

"Actually, you phoned just at the right time".

"To save you from something, something called Salome?".

He laughed lightly. "Yes, you could say that. Listen, I know this might sound a bit lame but I miss you. Tom keeps asking me when am I coming home. You see, I want to go home".

"So why did you leave?".

"You kicked me out, remember?".

"Yes, I remember very well, something called Tessa came between us".

"I didn't want a divorce".

"You didn't leave me too many options".

"I made a mistake. You couldn't forgive me".

"Did you expect me to. Why is it men think they must prove themselves, their sexual prowess".

"And women don't? It didn't take long before you were in bed with that old man".

"He was not an old man. He had charm, more than you ever had".

"Come on, he was more than old enough to be your father".

"Why should you care, what's it to you who I see or don't see. I don't see you acting like a monk".

The door to the lounge opened, Tom stood in his pyjamas with his cuddly penguin under his arm.

"Can I sleep with you in your bed?", he asked innocently.

"Do you know, Tom, I think that's a really good idea. You can sleep between mummy and me".

She turned, prepared to be angry, to contradict him, to ask him if he was mad. Did he really think she would slip into the bed where Salome had just been. He looked back at her and she could see a sign of despair in his eyes, a longing she had not seen for so long. She closed her eyes for a moment and tried to remember her feelings for the father of her child. Their passion, her love, which had turned to anger with a tinge of hate. The idea that he still loved her and the acceptance that she had never stopped loving him. Michael Lee had tried to smash her trust in those she loved, had loved. And here was Peter offering renewal of old love. She loved him, she had never not loved him.

"I agree with daddy. Let's all cuddle up together like we used to do but first I want to change the sheets".

He took her in his arms and she remembered how they used to love, his tenderness, his warmth. She felt a tear rolling down her cheek. She had lost him to some cheap pickup who had drawled down the back of his neck until he gave way. She could understand how it had happened, she had wanted to say it did not matter, but it did. Her pride had been irreparably damaged, so she had thought. He stepped back a little and saw the tear.

"Oh, Sophie, I never stopped loving you".

"I know. We'll take it a step at a time but for the moment, I'm going to crawl into your bed with a small buffer between us".

He smiled. "Come on, Tom, we've got some sleeping to do. Some catching up to do".

It was somewhere in the early morning hours when she woke up with a start. Michael Lee's remarks had hung on her, depressing her, she even thought she had dreamt about her mother and Monty's house but the dream evaded her. She stared up at the fluorescent stars and planets which Peter had stuck onto the ceiling to help Tom feel at home. It was then, suddenly, she remembered what had felt wrong, out of place, the last time she went to Monty's house to collect her clothes and whatever else she had left there. She had walked past the spare bedroom and noticed both duvets were turned back as though the bed had been slept in. She had noticed it but not registered it, not questioned why.

Now, as she laid in the dark room with Tom squashed in between she and Peter, she gasped at the idea of Monty and her mother sharing a bed when she was visiting. Surely, she thought, her mother had stayed at 'The Cutter'. Monty had told her he had booked a room for her. She felt smothered by doubt, fear and nausea, overcome by the need to find out anything she could. She could not leave it, accept it, the need to know was paramount.

She did not want to check up on her mother's visit to Monty, but she felt compelled to drive down to Monty's house and ask around. Maybe one of the neighbours knew something and then she would go to 'The Cutter' to scan the visitor's book. She thought she would rope Jillie in, perhaps she could attract the attention of the receptionist while she thumbed through the register. She might even be able to hide it under her coat and read it in the toilet. She thought that was an idea.

She realised how much of her mother was in her, fifty percent, and her curiosity was part of that fifty percent. She riled at the thought of inheriting those genes. The genes which made her mother so irritating. No, she did not want to be like her mother but she feared she was.

She glanced over to Peter who was awake.

"Can't you sleep?", he whispered.

"No, I'm thinking. I have a few things to do".

"Such as?".

"Nothing important".

He reached across and stroked her auburn hair. "You are so beautiful, Sophie. Please give me another chance. I am so sorry".

She turned her head. "You know what I like about you?".

"No, what?".

"Being able to say sorry. So few people can do that. They see it as weakness, I see it as strength".

*   *   *

Ann Bailey

A MULTIPLE OF LOVE

Helen BENNETT LIT A CIGARETTE and smiled broadly, amazed how easy it had been to arrange a date with Mike, which made her wonder whether she should be even more careful than she had planned to be. She decided they were similar, both capable of committing bad deeds, after all he had been willing to leave her to drown as she had Emy. It took one to know one.

Her anger had subsided, in fact now it was almost funny, he clicking an unloaded gun while she swam to the side of the lake. It would certainly have been poetic justice had she drowned. Now she had to decide how to pay him back, financially would be too difficult though she would love to clean him out. Perhaps, she could seduce him and drop him just when he thought she was in love with him. She thought that sounded juvenile, rather like a teenager plotting a vendetta in her bedroom between her discarded soft toys and Barbie dolls. However, she could not think of anything better.

She had called Sophie to tell her she was going to sell the cottage, a rather lame excuse. Then she dropped Mike's name and asked her for his address or telephone number. Sophie had readily given his mobile number, confirming her suspicion she had some kind of contact with him. In fact, Sophie having contact with Mike did not particularly worry her. She thought her own sexuality, as an older woman, was more powerful than any younger woman who might have wedding bells ringing in her ears which so often discouraged an undecided lover.

She met Mike as planned. He ordered oysters and she reminded him of how they were an aphrodisiac and purposely let the juice roll slightly down the side of her mouth. He had taken his napkin and gently dabbed the careless dribble and she had smiled, the kind of smile which spoke the unsaid word. He reacted magnificently and they spent the next two hours eating and drinking too much good wine until it was time to leave. They had taken a taxi to his apartment and had fallen on his crisp white sheets and made love as though their hunger had not been satisfied.

"I did not mean this to happen", she lied.

"I did", he replied, smiling the smile she had hated.

"Is Jack out of the picture?", he asked later, as she laid back smoking a cigarette, something he did not approve of in his house but let it go as part of the evening's entertainment, enjoyment.

"Yes, I guess so".

"Does that bother you?".

"Not any more", she laughed softly, as she turned and kissed his firm youthful body.

"That's okay then", he replied, kissing her breasts in return.

He smiled to himself as he pictured her as a sophisticated woman in the nineteen thirties, dressed in a slivery evening gown with an extremely deep cleavage and cut to the waistline at the back. A slender creature with a cigarette in a holder in one hand and a glass of champagne in the other.

He thought of the woman who had married a 'would-be' king, she must have had something about her. It was not her body, so what was it? He compared Helen to her as he passed his hand over her sparse breasts again.

'More than a handful is a waste', he thought, and he wondered if the Duke had thought the same about his Duchess.

*

She stood on the mooring one last time before locking up for the winter. She had intended selling the cottage but changed her mind at the last minute leaving behind an angry estate agent.

It was a place which held secrets, it had dominated her life, her emotions, her love for Jack. She could not let it go, one day maybe but not yet, for it was as though it pulled her, held onto her like the strangling waterweed. She even wondered if it would be the death of her as she watched the green water slowly turn black as the sun set.

She sighed as she remembered her feelings when she watched divers search for Rob under the melting ice. His face was deadly white and she had not dared to touch him, stroke his face, for she knew his body would be hard and unyielding. Her mouth turned down as she thought of him and small tears pricked her eyes as she allowed herself to admit that somewhere she missed him, perhaps because Jack had cooled off because he found it difficult to forgive himself, let alone her.

And then Rob's mother, Belle, who was found between the frozen reeds. Of course, she should have protected her but she really could not see the point of saving an old lady who would grieve for the rest of her life. After all, you put an animal down if it is in constant pain.

She looked back at the now deserted cottage where she had loved Jack, where she had schemed to keep him at whatever the cost and the cost had been high. Indecently high. She had not realised the full consequence of her jealousy. It had brought only unhappiness to her and everyone else involved. She tried to convince herself that she was not responsible. She had not killed anyone, at least not directly, rather not helped to avoid their deaths but not more than that.

She sighed again, she seemed to sigh a great deal nowadays, what was the good of all this sentimentality. Jack had cheated on his wife and now he boo-hoo'ed. She thought he should face facts,

Emy was dead and they were alive.

Luckily, Mike was in her life, which somewhat boosted her now low morale, lunching on a regular basis, a show in town or a film. She felt as though she was young again, being wooed for the first time though she was unsure whether she was enamoured because he made her feel special; attentive to her mood; the single red rose he left on her pillow; the special handmade chocolates or the expensive perfume. She loved romance, in fact, nowadays, she found it more important than the act itself for without romance sex was just another enjoyable pastime. Romance, she thought, took it a step further but she wondered how long she could keep him before he became tired of her, before some beautiful young girl crossed his path, though up until now he seemed quite happy with their arrangement. She could not understand how she could return his passion after she had secretly loved Jack so much, for so many years. A love she would have died for and she wondered if she would feel the same about Mike. Would she die of love for him. She thought not.

*

It was when her cold would not clear up, when her cough seemed almost chronic, when her weight loss was becoming unattractive, when her mouth felt sore, did she go to the doctor. He had given her a full examination and at the end looked at her puzzled and suggested an immediate blood test. She had known, instinctively known, that something was wrong and her thoughts jumped to every possible terminal illness.

"I'll phone you when I get the results. It might take a little longer than usual because I want to do a whole range of tests".

She had agreed to wait for his call and meanwhile she was get a lot of rest and not to have any sexual contact until she had heard from him.

Her mind raced to cancer of the cervix or the womb. She could hardly believe the doctor could be correct, he was just doing extra tests to be sure.

'Oh, God', she thought. 'I don't want to land up middle aged and sick, I'm not ready for that, I'm not ready to be ill. I'm not ready to die'.

Mike phoned her a few days later, he had not contacted her earlier and she had not cared.

"Listen,", he said, sounding apologetic, "I have to go to Singapore".

"Again? You've only just got back".

"Yes, I know, but I want to make an investment. Jimmy Lee has a couple of good leads. I'll contact you when I get back".

"Fine", she replied, sounding as depressed as she felt.

It was over a week before the doctor telephoned her. He wanted to see her. She tried to ease information out of him but he remained professional and said it was imperative she came to his office. Two days later, she sat opposite this serious looking man who seemed to avoid eye contact as he studied the papers in front of him. Eventually, he glanced up at her and then back down again to the papers.

"I'm afraid you have 'Hiv'. Try not to worry", he quickly added. "There's a lot we can do to help nowadays. Have you any idea who may have passed it on to you?".

"No", she gasped. "Though it could have been my husband. He died recently. I always suspected something was not quite right but I was never sure".

"Well, any partners you've had will have to be told and tested", he added.

"Yes, of course", she agreed, hardly listening to anything more he had to say.

She drove home in a daze, her mind racing as she tried to recall anything which might give her some clue as to who carried the illness, was it Rob, Jack or even Mike. Whichever one, Jack and Mike had to be informed.

She grimaced, if she sought to revenge Mike, then revenge she had. But Jack was now involved, that she felt would be the ultimate tragedy. And as for herself, well she really did not care that much for the joke was also on her.

She had never heard Jack so angry. He had shouted that Emy was bloody right, he should have listened to her. Everything which had happened was her fault, not his, and now this. He would like to wring her neck.

"I have to know if you are infected", she said quickly, aware their conversation was going to be short and sharp. He slammed down the telephone.

Well, she thought, that's the first, now Mike.

She knew she could reach him on his mobile but she had no desire to be screamed at again. She decided to send an email and hoped he regularly opened up his laptop. She sighed as she typed a small message.

"Mike, Something rather terrible has happened, please phone me immediately. It is very important you do so. Please take this mail seriously, you might be very ill. Helen."

She waited for a minute before hitting the 'send' button, sat back and waited for the next round of insults. Strange that, she thought, why should I get the blame. One of them gave it to me. One of them should be shouting at the other, not at me.

Mike returned her email. He had no time to 'phone at the moment but would do so as soon as possible.

She mailed back to say that she did not give a damn whether he contacted her or not. His health was his problem. She had warned him and, as far as she was concerned, she need do no more.

He sounded irritated when he eventually 'phoned her. Had he been kind, concerned, she would have put it differently, more diplomatically, but he had rubbed her up the wrong way and a familiar anger ran through her.

"You have to go to a doctor. You have to be tested"

"For what?"

"Hiv".

"What?".

"You heard what I said. I want to know who you've been with before me".

"I could ask you the same, bitch".

There was a silence.

"Are you there?", she asked, angrily.

"Yes".

"And?".

"I'll let you know".

"Do that", she shouted, slamming down the 'phone.

The hurt and insults hit her hard, first Jack and now Mike. They both blamed her, she was the common denominator, she was to blame. Neither of them commiserated with her situation, neither of them thought passed themselves. She hated them, she hated men.

She stared at the row of bottles on the kitchen table, barely able to believe that this was to be her life. Pills and yet more pills. Visits to doctors and blood tests.

*

She opened the front door to Jack a few days later. He brushed her aside, waving an envelope. "I don't have it, it's not me", he shouted. "Thank God I've not been with you for months. So who is it, who the hell have you been sleeping with?".

"What I do is my business. Aren't you overlooking the obvious".

"What obvious?".

"Rob".

"Rob", he repeated, as though amazed at such a plausible suggestion.

"Come on, Jack. You know as well as I do that Rob wasn't interested. I've always wondered if he was on two sides".

"He wasn't homosexual".

"How do you know that. Come in, I have to sit down. I'm worn out, I don't know what to do. We can just as well hate each other sitting down".

"I know", Jack almost spat out, as he followed her into the lounge, "because he told me something he never told anyone else, that's why I understood him. He relied on me and I tried to be there for him".

"What something?".

Jack flopped down in Rob's chair, the one he had sat on when he suggested they should go down to the cottage to skate. She was suddenly overcome by a feeling of sadness, just as she had done on the mooring at the cottage. She wondered if she was becoming soft, she hoped not. She would not know how to cope with those feelings.

"I need a whisky, with ice", he added.

She grudgingly fetched his drink feeling like a servant to a man she suddenly disliked. She was surprised at her feelings, how could she ever dislike Jack. Wasn't he her begin and end all to life, years of adoration. She could and would not stop loving him, she would reject any hidden anger.

"And you were saying?", she almost spat the words out.

Jack swirled the whisky and ice around in the glass before he took a mouthful. He let it linger for a few seconds, as if he was a connoisseur, before finally swallowing it. He repeated this ritual again as though to gain time before answering her.

"His parents sent him to a boarding school. More his father's idea than his mother's. He thought he was becoming a mummy's boy and needed toughening up. Well, that's not what happened. He was raped by some senior drunken bag of shit".

"Oh, no", she gasped.

"It broke him. His schooling became a disaster and, in desperation, he was brought home and sent to a local private school. Charles was teaching there. I don't know if his father guessed what happened. His mother certainly did not know. Anyway, he got through his education rather well but the experience ruined his life. He never recovered. He wanted a normal married life but he just couldn't get it together".

"Me, what about me?", she screamed. "He married me in the hope he could learn to screw".

She could feel the air leaving her lungs, feel and hear herself gasping for breath and for a second she saw Emy on the bed doing the same. Gasping for air, for life.

She ran to the bathroom and threw up over the toilet.

She heard Jack behind her.

"I'm sorry", he said. "You wanted to know. I never wanted to tell you. I promised Rob I would never tell anyone. It was not Rob who gave you Hiv, it's not me. So who the hell is it?".

"It's not your business", she gulped, as she rinsed water through her mouth. "You still can't be sure whether Rob found solace with another man".

"I'm one hundred and one percent sure Rob never looked at another man. He leaned on me, he looked to me for support, he did nothing without telling me", he said, sounding emotional.

"And you found that normal. Poor Emy".

"Poor Emy", he shouted, angrily. "What a pity you didn't think of that earlier".

"Yes, what a pity", she screamed back "You were not Rob's friend, you were his crutch. With you around he didn't have to get better, get on with life, you held him back. You helped him to ruin my life".

She was aware of a stinging pain as he hit her across her face and felt her ear ringing as she fell slightly backwards.

"I'm sorry, I'm sorry", he stuttered, his voice choking back yet more emotion.

She knew she was out of control when she beat him with her fists, tore at his shirt and scratched his face. She also knew their relationship was irrecoverably broken. He would go, never love her again. She felt tears streaming down her face though she was not aware of crying and her body shook as she semi collapsed, hoping he would catch her, hoping he would comfort her.

She heard herself give a pitiful cry, like an animal who had lost its mate, an animal in pain, but still he made no movement towards her.

"Get out, get out", she screamed, hysterically. "It was all for nothing, nothing".

There was a dreadful silence as he slowly turned around. "What do you mean by that? All for nothing?".

"I don't mean anything".

He grasped her arm tightly. "When I arrived Emy was nowhere near to the mooring. How could she have been so far away?".

"How should I know. She splashed around. How should I know".

"She was where she was because you pushed her there. You weren't saving Emy, you were helping her to drown".

He pinned her against the wall. "What did you do, what the bloody hell did you do?".

"She fell into the water, I tried to help her", she screamed, hysterically.

"You're lying. How could you, how fucking could you. I loved her", he choked, as he released his grip. He trembled as he leaned against the door frame. "How could you", he cried, as he sank down onto his knees.

"Please believe me. I would never have done that. I would never have hurt her".

She watched him from her lounge window as he walked, stooped, across the road and out of sight.

"What about me?", she screamed, unable to absorb the misery of a man who realised he had made love to a woman who only loved herself.

She fell into Rob's chair and wept uncontrollably at the deceit of Rob and the naivety of Jack, aware of the thin line between love and hate, for now she hated Jack as she had hated no one else. If Rob had only told me, she thought, I could have loved him. He had only to tell me, we could have worked things out. All that for nothing. All the years of blaming myself and then despising him, for nothing. What a waste, what a waste of our lives.

She sat down at Rob's desk, that evening, and gently swivelled the well worn leather office chair from side to side. Jack's story was foremost in her mind, she could not dismiss it, she had been hurt, angry and above all shocked. Jack and Rob had confided in each other, which did not surprise her for she had always viewed them as being over friendly, but she could never have guessed why.

She pulled out the narrow drawer in the middle of the desk where she knew there was an old mobile which Rob had used from time to time. She had cast it aside since it was too large and out of date to match her now rather chic wardrobe. She plugged it into a socket in the kitchen while she reluctantly made something to eat. She considered food to be a necessity, no more than that.

An advertisement on the television reminded her of the now charged 'phone. She really did not expect to find anything very interesting when she searched through it. However, there was just one number she could not place in the address book. A number without a name. She pressed the call button. Sam Somerford answered.

"Who is calling?", he asked, sounding surprised and perhaps concerned.

She quickly closed the mobile, both amazed and curious. He was Rob's financial advisor and she had visited his office, just once, to sell Rob's shares.

She had never met him before then, only knew of him. He had turned out to be a rather thin, sallow, looking man, his mousey brown hair streaked with grey, his forehead deeply lined above his almost invisible eyebrows. He had kept his light brown eyes cast down as he fumbled through Rob's portfolio.

"Sell it all. Lock, stock and barrel", she had instructed him, firmly shutting the door to any suggestions he might have to the contrary.

"If that's what you want", he had replied, sounding indifferent.

She told him how she liked to see her assets printed on a bank statement, preferably with a row of noughts. Not bits of paper informing her of the price of some commodity, or product, which could vary almost by the minute and which could burst like a bubble at the push of a button on some investment banker's computer.

She had left his office feeling strangely dissatisfied. He had noted her instructions and then shown her the door as though he had ended a job interview. He had avoided direct eye contact, had not tried to persuade her to keep at least some of Rob's shares, had kept their conversation short, not offered her tea or coffee, not asked her how she was managing, had written down her new address without commenting on how she lived in a nice area. In fact, she was out of his office almost before she had crossed her legs. She did not like him.

She had thought of Belle as she drove home in a taxi, a miserly old woman not like her husband Charles who was generous and rewarded her every year after their discreet holiday frolic. She was unsure whether Rob knew about his mother's hidden fortune, she thought not for he often slipped her small amounts of money.

"Buy yourself something nice", he would say fondly.

"You scheming old bag", she mumbled, remembering how Belle had let her house become dilapidated, refusing to have a home help or a gardener. Constantly complaining about being cold while she kept the thermostats on the radiators low. She was not sorry she had died and was happy she had been so 'careful' since it had gone towards an exclusive apartment near Hampstead Heath.

Now, she wondered if Somerford would return her call. She thought he might need some time to weigh up the pro's and con's, after all careful judgement was his business.

Fifteen minutes later the 'phone rang.

"I believe you've just called me, Mrs. Bennett, can I help you?".

"Yes, perhaps you can. I would like to see you. I was looking through Rob's papers again. I've been thinking, perhaps I should buy back some of the shares I sold when he died. That is, if they've dropped in price since then".

There was a silence before he answered.

"Yes, would you like to come to the office next Wednesday? I believe that is a quiet day. Actually, perhaps we could have lunch together".

A gut feeling ran through her as she hung up, he was far too friendly.

*

It was a miserable cold day when she met Somerford in a restaurant off Baker Street. He stood up as the waiter showed her to the table and gave her a limp handshake.

"So, have you any ideas on what you would like to invest in?", he asked, after ordering drinks.

"No, you're the expert. Actually, I am more interested in your friendship with my husband. Rob told me you went to school together", she bluffed, since she could not really remember any details.

He sat back in his chair and turned a knife over several times before answering.

"I suppose this is the real reason for your visit. What do you want to know?", he asked, sounding resigned.

"I believe my husband was ill, perhaps he

knew it. I would be grateful for your help. I have a problem".

"I'm sorry to hear that", he replied, looking at her directly. "He knew. I thought he had told you. I was not surprised to hear of his death. He was depressed. Didn't you notice?".

"No, I can't say I did. He went through the ice. Surely, that was an accident".

"Who knows".

She concentrated on a small silk flower arrangement on the table as she tried to recall the day Rob had suggested he should go down to the cottage to skate. She had not paid too much attention to his tone of voice or his mood. She thought he had seemed rather elated, not depressed as Somerford was now suggesting.

"When did you tell him?".

"About two years ago".

"So long ago and he didn't tell me", she gasped at the implications of such stupidity.

"Yes, that was remiss of him".

"Remiss. I would say criminal".

"Well, perhaps he thought it was time enough to tell you when you felt unwell. He probably hoped you hadn't got it. I really don't know".

"And if I had a friend?".

He smiled at her, whimsically. "I don't think he considered that an option".

Her anger rose at his subtlety. She had no intention of telling him anything about her private life. She controlled her desire to degrade him, suggest he sounded feminine and that only a bitchy

Ann Bailey

woman would talk like that, but instead she chose to ignore him.

"I believe you met at boarding school", she continued, still bluffing.

"Yes".

"Why did he leave?".

"He was expelled, we both were".

"Why?".

"We experimented. Boys do that, sometimes, you know".

"No, I don't know. Perhaps you would like to enlighten me".

He sighed and grimaced at the same time as he straightened the cutlery on the bright red table cloth.

"We were born like that. It is not a choice. Rob married you truly hoping he could turn it around. I accepted how I was. You must have known. I always expected you to divorce, you must have loved him very much not to have done so".

"I must have missed the telltale signs", she snapped, bitterly, as she lit a cigarette and blew the smoke towards his face before stubbing it out, since smoking was not allowed in the restaurant.

She hated his face, his glib manner. The idea of Rob being attracted to this rather pale, unappealing, man appalled her. She hated Rob now, more than she could ever have imagined. She felt she must have been aware that perhaps he had a dual sexuality but she had not wanted to know, not to have it definitely confirmed. Only when she was young did she have him followed for a few weeks but it had been an expensive business and she had given up. Perhaps the detective had followed him precisely the wrong weeks, perhaps Rob had a gut feeling he was being followed and was careful.

"Was it only you or were there others?", she continued, almost politely.

"As far as I know, only me".

"So how did it happen?".

"I went to the States. It was my fault. I had an affair. I carried it without knowing for years. I am really sorry".

"And what did Rob say. That's alright, old chap, I understand. I just happen to be married and have probably passed it on to my unsuspecting wife". She could hear herself shouting.

He put his hand over hers. "Let's go. My place is not too far from here. I'll get a taxi, we need to talk privately".

Her instinct was to walk away, to slap his face and go, but she wanted to hear more. She wanted to hear it all.

He lived in an expensive block of flats boasting a doorman and a thick carpeted elevator with mirrored walls.

The decor in his luxury apartment was carefully chosen with just a few ceramics and a couple of very modern pictures. It surprised her because to look at him one would think he was just another run-of-the-mill man with no particular aesthetic talent for design.

"How are you?", he asked, as though she had a simple cold or headache.

"How do you think I am. Frantic, desperate. Frantically desperate".

He did not answer as he walked into a shiny white kitchen and opened a large refrigerator.

"Wine?".

"No", she answered, shortly, for she did not think he deserved any unnecessary courtesy. He was the enemy who had infected Rob and perhaps, through her, Mike. "I heard Rob was raped by some senior bum at school. I suppose that's also a lie".

"Yes, it is".

"But his father knew the truth?".

"Yes, both our fathers were called to a meeting with the headmaster. Rob's mother was not there, it seems his father thought it unnecessary and my mother was away on holiday".

"But his mother was led to believe Rob was raped. Did she ever know the truth?".

"No, she would have been devastated. It was because of her he lived the lie. I am really sorry this has happened, that you have it".

"You talk of 'it' why can't you just say the word out loud. Say it for what it is. Hiv".

"If that makes you feel better, then yes, Hiv".

"Do you have any idea of what you have done?".

"Of course, I would be a moron not to understand the consequences. What can I say to make it different, to help you. I've tried to be honest. I hope you will take that into consideration".

"Yes, I'll give you that much".

"How did you know about Rob and me?".

"I didn't, there was a telephone number without a name and you didn't come to his funeral. I bluffed. I knew he had known you at school and his friend, Jack Nielson, told me some story of how he was raped. I just put two and two together. I would not have known if you hadn't told me. Thanks for that, if nothing else".

She got up to leave and turned as she opened the front door.

"I hope you feel guilty for the rest of your life".

"Don't worry, I'm sure I will. What about the new investments", he added, almost hopefully.

She gave a hard, pretentious, laugh. "Over my dead body".

He smiled, almost kindly. "Over our dead bodies, darling".

*

She emailed Jack when she got home. She thought it would do him good to know Rob, his confidant, his best friend, had lied to him for years. Had it never occurred to him that Rob's arm around his shoulder and his constant admiration were perhaps exaggerated. Perhaps there had been a touch of homosexuality about it. Had he really not noticed that. Had he been selectively blind to protect Rob's fine feelings, had that been more important than reality, her reality.

She went on to call him names and hoped he had a conscience. He had helped Rob to mislead everyone and, most importantly, her. As far as she was concerned, they could all rot in hell.

The internet was full of articles on Hiv and Aids. It seemed that some people were immune while others were not. Her occasional liaisons with Jack had lasted over a year whereas Michael Lee had been a constant lover for less than a year. Surely, she thought, it was not possible for Mike to become infected while Jack had not. There would be no justice if that was so.

It was some weeks before she heard from Mike. He emailed her saying he wanted to see her. He did not mention an Hiv test and a sickening feeling overwhelmed her for his message was not friendly, not that she had expected it to be. She did not reply to his mail, she thought it purposeless to do so. It would not change anything.

*

"I could kill you, you stupid bitch". His voice sounded cracked and sharp on her mobile. "I want to see you".

"Why, what good will it do? If you are positive then I am sorry. Believe you me I am sorry and I am also sorry for myself".

"I don't have the results yet. I have to be free of you for several months. You've had a life, mine is just beginning. It's not worth anything if I'm infected".

"That's not entirely true. You aren't the only one, there are tens of thousands of people in the same boat. You can still have a reasonably good life, meet someone, even if you're positive".

"I did meet someone, that's the problem. Do you see what you and your mucky crowd have done. Ruined peoples' lives".

"Are you coming here, or not?".

"Are you willing to take the risk that I might shoot you".

"I'll take the risk, what have I to lose", she whispered.

She clenched her jaw as she closed her mobile, burdened with guilt. How could she help him when she could not help herself. She even thought Mike would do her a favour if he put her out of her misery. It was true, she had lived her life, lived it badly.

It seemed that everyone she had loved now hated her and Rob, who she had learnt not to love, had cheated on her, not once but her entire married life. She felt a despair she had never felt before.

A despair which almost surpassed the loss of her almost stillborn baby.

She opened the glass doors of a cabinet displaying her special pieces. She wondered why she had collected valued items, items which did not add to the value of life.

"Everyone knows you can't take them with you, so why bother in the first place. What do I need them for, I never use them. I'm alone", she sobbed, pitifully, as she carefully lifted out a fine porcelain teapot, cup and saucer. She decided, as she walked to the kitchen, that she would use everything she owned, enjoy everything she possessed, and when they became boring she would sell them. All of them. And if they became damaged then, so what. Possessions were no longer important and she almost felt a sense of relief, a sense of freedom.

She found a packet of loose tea in the kitchen cupboard, then boiled a kettle of water, warmed the teapot as her mother had instructed her, and spooned the tea carefully into the pot. She was so careful, so precise, she felt as though she was performing an ancient tea ritual. Eventually, she poured the honey coloured tea into the cup and stared at the leaves floating on the surface.

"Things always get in the way", she murmured, as she carefully spooned them out and added the milk. "That's love, it never stays clear for long. Something always comes along to make it murky".

*

Mike arrived late as though staying the execution. There was no warm welcome only a bitter confrontation.

He pushed past her just as Jack had done, his face white with anger.

"Well", he shouted. "What have you to say for yourself. Who else did you sleep with apart from

Jack?".

"My husband".

"Other than Rob!", he shouted.

"Just Rob. What do you think of that. I am not the slut you would have me be. I found the culprit, Rob's old school buddy. Some gay who had an affair in New York. It seems he was infected for years without knowing. Rob caught it. End of story".

"Was Rob gay?", he asked, in disbelief.

"Seems so. I had my suspicions but I was never really sure. He covered it up well, I didn't realise he was on both sides. In the end I just thought his sex drive was limited, that maybe he was born like that. I thought he might have taken after his mother. His father told me she was cold".

"I've been with Jimmy Lee's granddaughter, Mia".

"Congratulations", she snapped.

"Well, you must have known we would not go on forever. You're old enough to be my mother".

"Thanks for that, Mike. I didn't notice you worrying about it".

"I didn't say I worried about it, I am just stating a fact".

"So, what about this new love in your life?".

He looked away.

"Did you take precautions?".

"No, she said she was on the pill".

"Does she know?".

"I haven't told her yet".

"You mean you left her, without saying anything?".

"I had to. I can't be around if she is positive".

"Why not?".

"What do you think her family will do to me?".

She felt suddenly sorry for him. "Try not to worry, from what I've read the chances of picking it up are quite small. Not everybody gets it. There's more than a good chance neither of you are infected".

She noticed how she called Hiv 'it', just like Sam Somerford. She felt almost sorry for Sam, of course he felt bad just as she did now.

"So what's next?", she pushed on.

"Nothing, I have to be free of you for some time before I can be finally tested. I can't go back", he added. "Whether she has caught it or not. I can't go back. God help me if she has it".

He walked to her refrigerator and poured himself a large glass of wine.

"I'll be in big trouble if her family find out. They will go ballistic, they will probably have me killed".

They sat until late, drinking and talking until eventually she went to bed and Mike laid along the sofa completely drunk. She kissed his forehead and he stirred a little as she covered him with a blanket.

"I still love you, Mike", she whispered. "I don't suppose you will ever forgive me".

*   *   *

JIMMY LEE

Jimmy LEE WAS IN HIS GARDEN practising Tai Chi before beginning his day. He believed this form of art kept his mind and body healthy. He had told his children, four beautiful girls, that they were to do Tai Chi every day and were to teach their children, his grandchildren, to do the same.

He looked up to see his daughter walking towards him.

"Ah, my dear child. What brings you here so early?".

"This man, Michael Lee. What do you know about him?".

"Only that I knew his mother long ago".

"You know Mia was seeing him".

"Yes, my lovely granddaughter, Mia. Is there something wrong?".

"He has dropped her. No goodbye. Left the country without a word. She is heartbroken. He told her he would work for you and then ask us if they could marry".

Jimmy pulled a towel from the back of a garden chair.

"I don't understand. He left without saying?".

"Yes, and I'm left with a daughter who won't stop crying. I think she has been to bed with him. I'm not sure but I think it very likely".

"There has to be a reason".

"Whatever it is, she won't tell me. I am worried there is more to all of this".

Jimmy Lee put his arm around his daughter,

"Try not to worry. I will ask Chia to see what he can find out. Is she having a baby?".

"No, I am sure she is not, thank God".

"Go home now and don't talk to anyone else about this".

Linda kissed him lightly on the cheek. "I will let you know if I find out anything, maybe she will tell me more". She bowed slightly as she left. "Thank you, dear father".

Jimmy Lee frowned as he walked slowly into his house. Why would a young man suddenly drop his beautiful granddaughter. A young woman who had everything to offer him. A chance to return to his own country and settle down with excellent prospects in his company. What would make him leave so quickly.

He picked up the 'phone. "Chia, I want you to do something for me. I want to know everything you can find out about Michael Lee. You met him once, he was with my granddaughter. I want to know every 'phone call he made and every 'phone call he received. I want to know who he saw and when he saw them. I want to know where he is now and every move he makes. I don't care how long it takes or how much it costs. Do you understand?".

He hung up. Chia was a thorough investigator, if there was something to find then he would find it.

It was nearly a week later when Chia handed Jimmy Lee a list of telephone calls. Only one was to London. The others were to Mia except for one to a Clinic.

"What clinic?".

"A clinic for Hiv, Aids".

Jimmy gasped, his face whitened and his lips formed a tight thin line.

"Do you know why he 'phoned them?", he asked, in a trembling voice.

"No, they won't give any information. I've tried to bribe them, even threaten them, but I have to be careful. I don't believe they will talk".

"Do you know where he is living?".

"He has an apartment in London but seldom uses it. He seems to spend his time with a Helen Bennett. An older woman who also lives in London and owns a small cottage in the country".

Jimmy Lee swivelled his chair around until he faced the windows. He stared out at the high rise buildings all reflecting the sun, all reflecting wealth.

"Find out more, see if he visits hospitals or doctors. Find out if he takes any medicines. I want to know everything about him. Then, when we are ready, we will ask him a few questions. I want him watched day and night. Arrange it".

He picked up his 'phone when Chia had left.

"Linda. Mia needs to be tested in a couple of months time".

"What for?".

"Hiv".

He heard a gasp, almost a small scream.

"Just to be safe", he added, softly. "Try not to worry. I still have to find out the details. Maybe, there is nothing to worry about. You don't have to tell her yet but make sure she does not have any new boyfriend. We will have to wait for just a little while".

He heard his daughter cry and he hung up quickly. He could not cope with such unhappiness. First, he must find out if Michael Lee was infected and, if he was, did he know it when he took his granddaughter out. If he did, then it was tantamount to murder and he would be dealt with accordingly.

He stared at the glittering buildings, it had so changed since he was a young man and in love with Jade. He wondered how Michael Lee, who could have been his son, had come to this.

He closed his eyes and let himself return to over thirty years ago when the old shop houses were being demolished to make way for high rise offices, shiny glass towers where stocks and shares were exchanged. A time when Singapore was emerging, becoming a city of entrepreneurs, a centre of commerce, bankers, brokers, traders, leaders in technology.

He was already married with a family of young

children when he met Jade. She was so beautiful, so incredibly beautiful. Her features chiselled, her movements elegant, her thoughts still pure but exciting. How could he not love her as she did him. He had promised to marry her, to leave his wife. He wanted to do that, though he doubted it would happen for there were too many family ties, too much family money, to extricate himself without causing a turmoil. Then, it was as though some ancient family spirit came to his help, came to free him from the web he had spun, he became ill. He did not even know he was sick until he had a medical check up for a new insurance policy.

He had tuberculosis. He could not believe it, he had nearly no symptoms, just a little tired. No more than that. His father had immediately arranged for him to go to Switzerland for treatment. He had not argued and he was gone within two weeks. He had barely said goodbye to Jade. Just a telephone call to tell her he would send a servant with money to help her settle down and that she must go to the doctor to be checked for tuberculosis. He was sorry, he was sorry. He had heard her crying and he had put down the telephone and wept. He never saw or heard from her again and he had not tried to find her.

Then, recently, her son had contacted him. He did not even know she had a son and concluded she had married and perhaps lived somewhere on the island. But it seemed the young man was living in England. He agreed to meet him for he was keen to hear what had happened to his old love, his Jade.

He had liked Michael, he had introduced him to his family and his granddaughter had been attracted to him. He seemed well educated, polite, charming. He had been shocked when he heard Jade had said he was his father. He had assured him how that was impossible and even offered to have a dna test which the unhappy young man had reluctantly accepted. Of course, he was not his father.

He had been disappointed that Jade had found another lover within a few weeks of his leaving the island. He thought she must have acted on the rebound and remembered how she had sobbed when he told her their affair was over. He carefully studied her son's features and recalled their European friends at the yacht club.

He had offered Michael a job in his company. After all, he had pointed out, he had no one in England since his mother had died. He had relations here and he thought it a good idea to look them up and even get to know his own family.

But, in spite of his kindness, Michael Lee had shown himself to be treacherous. He could never forgive that, never.

It was another two weeks before he heard from Chia. Indeed, Helen Bennett and Michael Lee had visited a hospital together. Chia's agent had managed to bribe a local chemist as to the pills they were taking. He had slipped him 'an envelope' and the chemist had discreetly written down names of pills, all were for a Mrs. H. Bennett. The medicines were antiviral.

"You mean they are used for Aids", Jimmy had asked, his voice sounding low and almost guttural.

"Probably, Hiv. The fact that only the woman is taking them suggests he is not infected or, of course, he might be waiting for test results".

"The next step is to get hold of the little bastard and question him".

"I'll see what I can arrange".

"Let me know".

He sighed deeply as he 'phoned his daughter when Chia had hung up.

"Linda, any news yet?".

"They tested her just to make her feel better, give her some hope. But they will have to wait a bit longer to be sure".

"How is she?".

"In a bad state. I had to tell her. She says she will kill herself if she has Aids. I am trying my best to keep her spirits up".

"He won't get away with this. I will make sure he regrets the day he set foot in my house. I will revenge her", he hissed.

*

It was another two months before Linda telephoned him. He swivelled his chair so that he could stare at the other skyscrapers and the ribbons of blue sky between them.

"Pa, she is totally clear. She hasn't got it, she hasn't got it", she gasped with happiness. "Lex said we are all to go on holiday. I can't tell you our relief.

Poor Mia, she has so suffered but we tell her it is behind her and one day she will meet a good man who is known within our circle. A man from a good family".

"We will celebrate", he laughed, loudly. "We will have a party before you go. It is good you take her away. It was a hard lesson".

They chatted on for a while and eventually his elated daughter said goodbye and thanked him for all the support he had given the family.

He redialled when she had hung up.

"Chia, I want to know if he is infected and, whether he is or not, I want you to make sure he never enters this country again. Give him a clear message that he is not welcome here, ever. No need for extremities but the message must be clear. Do you understand what I am saying?".

Chia replied that he understood very well what had to be done and would arrange for his wishes to be carried out. Coincidentally, there was a Chinese restaurant opposite his flat. It would be easy to arrange.

*   *   *

TWO OF A KIND

Helen HELD MIKE IN HER ARMS. He had wept when he received the results of his test. He feared for the future and the girl he might have infected. She wished she could think of something to say to help him but there was nothing. She felt empty and for the first time without a plan, any plan. Useless idioms and clichés rushed through her mind, fruitless remarks which would not add to his situation, their situation.

They curled around each other at night and she wished they could be found like that. Together in death, for her love had been fatal. She had wanted to shout to God, why had he done this to her, had she not suffered enough in a loveless marriage, a childless marriage. She recalled, as she so often did, her child born only to die minutes later. The tiny limp body of their baby boy had been taken away before she had a chance to hold him. It was like that in those days. Babies were not held by their parents with love until they slipped away. Such an infant death was something not to be spoken about after the first sympathetic words from family and friends.

Rob had seemed just as devastated as she was. He had held her in his arms and cried. She had never seen him cry before, she had not expected that.

She had sat days in a rocking chair clutching a finely knitted baby shawl. It was weeks before she could bring herself to carefully pack the tiny clothes between tissue paper, dismantle the cot and return it with the pushchair to the baby shop, which guaranteed their return in case of such tragedies.

Later, Rob had taken her away for a month to Fiji and she had managed to block the hurt and even enjoy herself for a while. They never spoke of the child again. It was as though their pain was buried with him, an unspoken subject, almost a taboo.

Rob's coolness continued and she slowly learnt to accept her marriage for what it was though she hoped, someday, someone would charge into her barren life. But no suitor arrived and she spent her time sewing patchwork quilts and sketched the colourful world around her.

She turned slightly and studied Mike who had fallen asleep. A lock of his thick dark hair fell across his forehead, his skin smooth but pale, his long lashes outlining the shape of his eyes, he was beautiful, so beautiful.

*

It was a cold miserable evening when Michael Lee left his apartment to go shopping. He often stayed with Helen but he was slowly trying to pick up his life and had returned to his own apartment. Sometimes, he ate in a small Chinese restaurant opposite but tonight he would go shopping to fill his almost empty cupboards and refrigerator.

He was thinking of Mia and whether he should contact her and tell her about the trouble she might be in. He thought he should do that, in fact he knew he had to do so, but he was overwhelmed by fear of her family and certainly her grandfather. He decided he would email her that evening, it was the only decent thing to do.

He was walking down the almost deserted street towards the supermarket when he became aware of someone behind him, he turned to see two men closing in on him. His heart was beating fast as he hastened his step and began to run but the men quickly caught up with him. He felt a man's arm around his neck and his left arm pulled behind his back while the other man hit him violently in the stomach. He gasped in pain and tried to bend over but the first man still held him tightly.

"Talk", the second man said.

"What about?".

"Your illness. Somebody wants to know when you knew you had it".

"What illness?".

"Don't mess around if you want to live".

"After I arrived in Singapore", he gasped. The second man punched him between his legs and he groaned in agony as they semi dragged him along the road and down an alley. He knew where he was. It was a side entrance to the Chinese restaurant.

"When did you know you were infected?", asked the man again.

"I told you, after I arrived in Singapore. I got an email from someone who had just found out she had it. I 'phoned her and she told me I could have Hiv. I mailed back to say I was leaving and that I would get tested at home. I left. I went home".

"Can you prove that?".

"The mails are on my computer".

"We will go to your flat. We will see if you are lying and if you are, you're as good as dead"

"I swear to you I'm not lying".

They pulled him across the road and he hoped there would be someone in the lobby and that they would run off, but there was no one in sight as they took the lift to his apartment. They hit him on the jaw as they flung him down in his lounge.

"Find it", the first man shouted as he crawled to his laptop.

"There", he gasped, pointing at the screen. "I told you. I'm not lying".

One of the men took out a mobile and dialled as he walked away, speaking softly in Chinese so that he could not hear what he said. When he returned he pulled him up by the collar of his coat.

"Be warned", he spat, his spittle wetting his face. "If you return to Singapore, that will be the last thing you ever do. Understand?".

He nodded then received one more blow in his ribs and another to his jaw.

"You are being watched, do you understand?. Every move, every telephone call, everyone you meet. Everything you do. We have our agents everywhere. If you go back to Singapore, you are dead. Understand?".

"Yes", he groaned.

He remained bent double for some time as an excruciating pain throbbed throughout his body.

He ran his tongue along his bleeding gums to check none of his teeth were loose or broken, then he slowly reached for the telephone. He wanted Helen, she was the only one who could help him. His mother and Monty were dead. He had no brothers or sisters. No close friends he could confide in. He had no one apart from her, the woman he had intended to destroy was now his only friend.

Helen was lying along the sofa with a glass of wine in her hand thinking, as she always did, about the past. About all that had happened and how she had failed in just about everything she had ever done or wanted to do, everything she had wanted to achieve. She had nothing, she did not even think she deserved to have anything.

Her telephone rang and she picked it up thinking is was some 'cold call' for she could not think of anyone else who might want to contact her.

Mike was on the other end of the 'phone. She sat up aware that his voice sounded strange, that something was very wrong.

"What is it?".

"Can you come, I can't drive. I'm unwell".

"What do you mean unwell?".

"I'll tell you when I see you", he choked.

"I'll be with you".

*

She gasped when she saw him sitting on his now blood stained sofa. He looked up at her, rather like a puppy which had been hurt.

"What happened, for God's sake", she cried, as she ran to him and put her arm around his shoulder.

"I think I got a visit from Jimmy Lee's friends. They warned me not to return to Singapore. I guess my leaving suddenly made them suspicious. They have probably been checking up on me".

"And what is there to check?".

"Not much, only that I 'phoned a Clinic but I didn't go. I decided to come home to get checked. I've no doubt they know I did that. They wanted to know when I knew I had Hiv and I told them it was after you mailed me. They dragged me here and I had to show them your emails. Thank God I could prove I was telling the truth. I don't know what would have happened if you had 'phoned me instead. Then one of the men made a call and afterwards they beat me up a bit more and warned me never to return to Singapore. I think Mia must be in the clear. That's all that matters. I think I would already be dead if she had caught it", he cried, slightly, as he spoke.

"You're not staying here. Come on, we're going home.

*

Mike looked distraught when he gave up his job and sold his apartment. He was now living with her and would not leave the house without her She tried to convince him that nothing more would happen, he had been warned and that was it. Obviously Mia was in the clear and her family were probably only too happy to forget about the whole ghastly affair. He should see it as an incident best put behind him and try to make something of what he had. Medicines were improving and he was lucky, he was rich. What about those who had nothing, who most probably would never have anything. What about them?

*

They were at the cottage in the early summer when he told her he was frightened to return to his own country and had only a work permit to stay in the U.K., for however long it might last.

"I have nowhere, I belong nowhere. I have no family, I have no country".

"Did your mother take her citizenship here?".

"Yes, Monty thought it wise to do so".

"But you didn't".

"No, I wasn't sure what to do, so I did

nothing. We never discussed it seriously".

"Well, I suggest you apply for it".

"It will take years", he whined, miserably.

She sighed at the new problem facing him and felt even more responsible for his position. She stared across the lake, it was a beautiful day, small fish came to the surface causing circles on the almost still water and once in a while a dragonfly darted through the reeds.

"There is a possible solution, don't be shocked, it's only an idea".

"What?".

"We could marry. Should anyone ask, we can say we have known each other since you arrived here and I knew your mother from years ago. My husband died. I was alone, you were alone. We fell in love. Simple".

He looked staggered, staring at her as though he had not heard her correctly. She waited for him to react, perhaps sneer at such an unlikely suggestion. Instead, he grinned broadly.

"Brilliant, truly ingenious. Why didn't I think of that. Would you really do that for me?".

"Yes, of course. Why not? Listen, I don't know the law, it could be that getting married does not necessarily mean you are entitled to become British, but I would say you have a pretty good chance. After all, your mother had a British passport, you studied here, worked here, lived here for a long time then you married a British citizen. You have a very healthy bank account, reasonably independent. That must say something, that must help".

"And don't forget Monty was my father",

She frowned. "Of course", she replied, thoughtfully. "I completely forgot about that. Only how can you prove the dna is from him. It could be from some other man. I mean he's dead.

"Yes, I can see that's a problem. It might not work. We'll stick to our plan, we can always try later if we have to".

"You don't have to marry me if you don't want to", her voice broke as she spoke.

He took her hand. "I can't think of anyone I would rather be with. You are so kind, so caring".

She looked away as tears ran down her cheeks.

"No one has ever said that to me. I am so afraid you don't mean it".

"I mean it, Helen. Maybe I don't need you to get a passport, I don't have the answer to that. But I do know we are two of a kind, we need each other, for better or worse", he laughed.

She dabbed her eyes with a tissue. "You know we have enough money to do nice things, go to nice places, live it up a bit", she added, softly. "That is, if you want to stay with me for a while".

"I can't think of anywhere else, or anyone else, I would rather be with. You are beautiful, Helen. We can make something of it, of life. Thank you for being so kind to me. Strange Monty helped my mother, now you are helping me".

She laughed as she began to cry again.

"You know, we could have an extended honeymoon. Get away from here. I think I will keep

Hampstead Heath and sell this place. Too many unhappy memories here".

"I'll put the beach house up for sale, same reason. Too many unhappy memories".

"You know what, we could go away every winter to somewhere warm".

"A lot of people go to Thailand", he said, thoughtfully. "It's so full of tourists, no one will notice us".

"Can you imagine months on a beach".

"Yes, I can. And the food is to die for", he grinned at his play on words which applied to his situation, their situation.

"We would have to take a supply of pills", she laughed through her tears.

"Yes, I guess so", he agreed. "We could also get married on the beach", he suggested, teasingly.

She looked up surprised. "What a lovely idea. We could ask a couple of passersby to be witnesses".

"Another problem solved. I really wouldn't know who to ask".

"Neither would I".

"Yes, that's what we'll do. Marry on the beach on Christmas Day".

"And if the paperwork is too difficult, then we'll marry here and still have Christmas somewhere on a beach in Thailand". She pulled the weekend newspaper off the coffee table. "Holidays", she murmured, as she thumbed through the paper. "Here we are. Thailand. Let's see. Phuket".

"That's the place to go. I've heard it's a very broadminded destination".

"Well, then, that's where we'll go".

"Thailand, here we come and when we get back I will look for a job and get my life together".

"Let's drink to that", she suggested.

He raised his glass. "To our new life", he toasted.

She sat next to him, her head resting on his shoulder.

"Did you really hope I would drown when you held the gun to my head and forced me to jump into the lake?", she asked.

"Did you guess Emy might die because you didn't take her to hospital?".

She paused for a moment, a little shocked at his direct question.

"I think there was a madness in me. I was desperate to be loved. I did not think further than myself. I've changed. I would die for you, I thought I loved Jack like that, but now I know I didn't love him. He was a sort of trophy, a sort of 'have to have'. I turned to him just after we were married, when I realised Rob was all about nothing".

She drunk some wine to give her support.

"But, true to form", she continued, "Jack was so-called loyal to his best friend. Perhaps it would have been better if we had just had a passionate affair and got all the feelings out of the way. I thought of him just about every day of my life and when we eventually met up again, he was married. He became a challenge. Pity Emy was such a nice person, it would have been so much easier if she had not been so"

"So what are you saying, you left her to die?".

"No, not that. I just didn't want to admit to myself that she needed to go to hospital. I suppose it was a sort of power struggle. I just couldn't get my brains in a row, I didn't, couldn't, think straight. That's what love does, makes you a bit mad".

"Well, we all do stupid things, who am I to judge. I nearly fucked up Mia's life and almost left you to drown. I don't suppose I am much better", he replied, not adding that he was also partly responsible for his mother's suicide.

"I hope not. I hope you are as bad as me. If not, then we will probably start playing the 'better than thou' game".

"I'm not very good at playing games. I like to win".

"Do you feel you have won now?".

"Sort of. I have you, haven't I?".

"Forever and ever".

He looked across the still lake and imagined Emy sitting on the mooring, dabbling her feet in the green water. He had not revenged her as he had intended. In fact, he was sharing the enemy's bed. He needed Helen, at this moment in his life. He had not forgotten all that had happened, nor the fact that it was because of her he was sick now.

"You know", he said, softly. "Perhaps we shouldn't sell the cottage or the beach house just yet. Prices are still rising. We can always do that later".

"Whatever you think best", she whispered.

She kissed him and for the first time it was a kiss of affection, as a mother kisses her child.

A kiss for her baby who had not lived long enough to know love, a kiss for her baby who had escaped the pain of life. A kiss which broke her heart.

*   *   *

JACK

It WAS SOME TIME BEFORE Will Windsor saw Jack sitting on a bench by the 'Crossing' with a black Labrador dog sniffing around nearby.

"Jack, Jack Nielson", he called. "How are you doing?".

He had invited him for a coffee and he could see how Jack reluctantly accepted. He was not surprised for he could imagine Jack might not want to be confronted with anyone who might know about him and Emy and their past.

Poppy had just come downstairs, still in her housecoat, and talked her usual rubbish, this time about Arnold Waters. He tolerated Arnie to please Rosie but he guessed, as did Poppy, that Arnie would disappear once someone to his liking walked into his life. Still Arnie was the instigator of his beautiful garden and had designed the rockery which everyone admired, along with the greenhouse which nurtured plants, the biological vegetable plots and the shed where he sold the produce along with brightly coloured Feng Shui pots. All this made Arnie a small profit and drew in more customers for he and Rosie. He thought he owed something to him and tolerated his expensive new ideas and he certainly owed something to Rosie who was now acting like an overgrown schoolgirl.

"And here she is", he muttered, as Rosie came through the back door with a bunch of flowers.

"Oh, Jack", she exclaimed. "How nice to see you. Have you seen our new conservatory and garden?".

"Yes, Will showed me and I've just had a quick coffee. I have to be off because of Vici", he added, trying to make a getaway.

"I'll walk with you, I have to put some flowers on the tables outside", she stated, walking into the garden.

"Actually", he said, having given up the idea of escaping from her. "I've been meaning to 'phone you, I want to thank you for being such a good friend to Emy. She didn't know too many people, we probably shouldn't have moved down here".

"So many people do that", she replied, sounding irritated. "Reach retirement and then move away from where they have lived for years. I don't know what they are thinking. The grass is seldom greener on the other side. It's difficult making a new life when you're older. Will wanted to move. I dug my heels in the local mud. Over my dead body, I told him", she stopped for a moment remembering how it was over a dead body. Will's father's body.

She cleared her throat. "Well, anyway, yes. We did build up a friendship".

"I guess she told you about us".

"A little, not as much as you might think. She loved you too much to say anything bad about you. You were a lucky man to have such a loving wife".

Jack hung his head and studied the path.

"You're right, Rosie", he said, bravely. "I wasn't there for her. I didn't protect her", he murmured.

"It wasn't your fault. These things happen. She believed in an afterlife. Perhaps she is with you, watching you".

He wanted to say, 'God, I hope not' but instead he managed a small smile. "You never know. I'll have to behave myself".

Rosie gripped his arm. "I shouldn't tell you this but I've seen her. By the bench at the 'Crossing'. She was sitting there, as large as life. Then she smiled and disappeared".

Jack stared at her to see if she was taking some pleasure in shocking him but he could not see anything in her expression or voice to support that.

"That's a nice thought", he replied, clearing his throat, again. "Something special I should say. I hope she's at peace", he added, lamely.

He wanted to tell Rosie that he had also felt a presence by the 'Crossing' and that Vici always growled at nothing when he sat there.

"It's a very special place", she continued.

"Yes, I believe Emy told me it was a pagan worshipping site until a Christian monk pinched their land".

Rosie stepped back slightly. "Well, not exactly. But I guess something like that. Did she tell you that there are lights there at night. I can see them from the tower in my house".

"Yes, she mentioned it. Hope to see you again soon", he murmured, quickly backing away

"Emy is still around, remember that", she called, as she left to go back into the house. "You will probably see her one day. Probably at the 'Crossing' or walking your dog across the heath".

Rosie smiled as she entered her beautiful conservatory. She had done exactly what she intended. Jack would always look over his shoulder, he would never be sure if he was being watched. She would try to contact Emy tonight when Will was asleep. The shadow which passed at the end of her bed, it was either Emy or Reginald. She liked to think it was Emy.

Will watched Rosie talking to Jack who fidgeted until he eventually broke away and quickly strode over the small paths between the heather towards his house. He doubted he would see him again in the near future.

He went into the garden and asked his customers if they were satisfied, could he refill their teapots, whatever. Poppy was tidying up the kitchen when he returned. He had forgiven his wayward mother who was not only in her element but, diplomatically, kept out of their way in the evenings by retiring to her rooms and watching every sitcom imaginable. It seemed to Will that they had all settled down to a rather nice life style, without debts and the weight of an old house pushing down on his shoulders, all thanks to his mother. All in all, he felt content, except for the fact his father was under the rockery and poor Emy. He thought she did not deserve to die when she did, she was far too young, far too bright and active. He thought life was cruel.

*

Jack hurried back over the heath trying, unsuccessfully, to forget the past and even considering whether he should move away from the area. He knew he needed someone, something, to fill his life and Vici did not do that. It was a nice dog, a friendly dog, but he slobbered leaving wet streaky lines on his trousers and had a rather demanding character. He thought he did not really have the patience for an animal and felt guilty thinking as he did. However, he had given the dog a good home and Vici was lucky not to have been put down after a too long stay in the kennel.

He could see a black form sitting astride a motorbike in his driveway. He frowned, he could not think who it could be. The form took off its black helmet and medium length blonde hair straggled down a woman's face. A woman with a motorbike was not in his address book, not that he knew.

"Jack Nielson?".

"Yes".

"Don't you recognise me".

"Have we met?".

"I think you could say that".

He recognised the voice. "Charlene?".

She smiled as he recognised her. "Yes, me".

He felt stunned and slightly worried, something between happiness and dread. He had left her to go abroad. He really had no option, anyway they were far too young. He could not possibly get tied down at the age of twenty, though they had been going out for more than two years and he realised she expected to get engaged and all that followed. His new job had arrived exactly on time, the opportunity to work overseas and to break with Charlene. After all, he told her, he had to consider his career and how could their friendship go further without him first building his future. She had cried, he had expected that, but he had firmly kissed her goodbye and promised to write. Well, he did write a few times.

He invited her into the house for a beer and talked briefly of the past. Then she kissed him. He could recall the warmth of her body against him, recall the feel of her when she was young, their secret lovemaking. He remembered how she had sat behind him on his motorbike, hanging on to his jacket while he showed off as he took the corners too sharply or swerved between the traffic. They had biked around the countryside until they came across some nice little dale, a clearing in a corpse, a trickling stream. It had been romantic but he never forgot to be careful, he was very aware of that. His father had just once broken the ranks of his stuffy, stiff, fellow peers who were almost unable to say the word 'sex', though he reckoned most of them would grab an opportunity if offered by some willing female, assuming they would not be caught, so long as they could get away with it.

His father had handed him a book on reproduction and, at the last minute, confided in him. It was probably the biggest secret the man held and he had divulged it in a moment of confidence.

"Your mother and I had to get married".

He could hardly believe his ears.

"It was not the best way to start a marriage. Be careful", he had warned.

It had been the first time his father had shown any signs of being less than perfect. He wanted to shout 'Hurray. Good for you', but he kept quiet to help his father retain his dignity.

"I'll be very careful", he promised, sincerely.

And he was, except for his affair with Jade when, for some reason or another, he loved with abandonment until he managed to get his brains in a row. He cooled off and she dropped him. He could not blame her, he had not been very diplomatic.

He was more careful after that though Emy had become pregnant. Strange that, he thought. She was on the pill, she swore she had taken it, she said it must have been an upset stomach though, in truth, he could not remember her having had one. He thought she had conned him but he had no option other than to accept the growing foetus and hope it would not happen again.

Luckily Charlene, who now called herself 'Charlie', was too old for that which was a plus point since young women were unpredictable, if they thought they were about to lose their lover. He had fleetingly considered rejecting Charlie but, on the spur of the moment, he had suggested they went down to the beach house and stay the night and perhaps the next day they could walk along the beach. Charlie had jumped at the idea.

He had taken her upstairs to find some underclothes which the girls always left behind. She had pulled two pairs of panties from out of a drawer together with the top Emy had died in. He had kept it. He could not bear to throw it away and he had been startled when she held it up

"Sweet Dreams" she had read out loud. "How cute".

In fact, it had been Helen's and he remembered how she had worn it on the weekends when he and Emy had stayed at the cottage. How she had come down the stairs into the lounge almost showing the tops of her legs, almost to the point of exposure. Emy had ignored it because she considered Helen rather plain and certainly not sexually dangerous. It was only later did it dawn on her that the so-called quiet ones, even the so-called plain ones, were just as dangerous.

"I'm sorry, I would rather you didn't take that one, there must be another".

She looked at him a little surprised and guessed it had some kind of sentimental value.

"Okay. What about this one?", she suggested, holding up a plain unadorned shirt.

"Yes, that's fine".

The ride down to Devon had been stressful. He had swerved between the traffic and dangerously overtook whenever he could, while Charlene hung onto his jacket as though her life depended on him, closing her eyes in fear and probably wishing she had not agreed to his racy invitation.

He had already regretted asking her to go with him by the time they both wearily stepped down off the bike and straightened their stiff backs.

"It's lovely here", she said, watching the sand as it blew across the beach and gulls swooping overhead. "Is it yours?", she asked, looking up at the little house.

"No, it belongs to a friend of my daughter, well actually my stepdaughter, the same thing", he answered, as he inserted the key in the kitchen door.

He tried to turn it, took it out and tried again but there was no movement in the lock. "Strange", he remarked, as he walked around to the patio and held his hand against the window so he could see in. The room looked empty. No trainers untidily thrown on the floor, no beach towels drying on the backs of chairs. Nothing except for a couple of armchairs and a coffee table. By this time Charlene was standing on the dunes staring down the beach.

"I'm just going to 'phone Sophie", he shouted to her, sounding worried.

He walked to where the dunes sheltered him from the wind and dialled her number.

"Sophie, I can't get into the beach house".

"No, Michael Lee has changed his mind", she answered, bitterly. "We can't use it anymore".

"I think he's changed the lock".

"Yes, he said he would".

"Why, what happened?".

"I have to go. I'll 'phone you back. What are you doing there? You didn't say you were going".

"I know", Jack replied, shortly. "I'll speak to you tomorrow evening".

He hung up quickly. He did not want to go into details.

"Sorry. Charlene, change of plans", he shouted, as he walked towards her. "The owner has decided to sell the house. I didn't know, seems he told Sophie. We'll try 'The Cutter'. Nice little pub in the village. I've been there with Emy".

He knew it was unfair to mention Emy's name, it could spoil Charlie's expectations of the night ahead.

*

The Bar was full of local people and holiday makers when they arrived.

"You'll have to wait", the barman told them when they asked for a table. "We're real busy tonight".

Jack's enthusiasm waned yet more as Charlene signed the hotel register, grinning as though she had won the lottery.

"I didn't ask you your surname", he remarked, reading 'C. Redman' as she wrote her name in the hotel register.

"We haven't actually discussed anything about each other. You could be a serial killer for all I know", she laughed, perhaps nervously.

"You never know", he replied, as they pushed their way through to the noisy bar and ordered drinks. He watched the congenial barkeeper while Charlene brought him up to date with her life. He listened, vaguely, while he thought of the weekend he and Emy had spent together at the beach house. He knew he could have been kinder, warmer. He wished he had apologised for all the misery he had caused, made it up properly, loved her as she wanted to be loved. But he could not love unconditionally, that was not who he was. He had always drawn lines and set down markers. He realised how tolerant Emy had been, to accept him on his terms.

He did not want to remember his last meeting with Helen, he did not want to know what happened the day Emy died. He did not want to know whether Helen was trying to drown her. He did not want to remember Helen, at all. Now he was drowning in guilt. Floundering in hopelessness. Not caring if he did not wake up. He was already in hell and he did not believe it would ever be different.

He thought of Rob, someone he also did not want to think about. He would, normally, have felt sorry for Helen but that was now impossible. He thought they deserved each other. Any sympathy he might have felt for either one of them had now turned to contempt.

He turned his attention back to Charlene who was now planning the next day. They would have a walk down the beach, then stroll through the village and then take a light lunch. Then they would go home to his place and, maybe, she would stay the night with him. Of course, she would eventually take him home to meet her children.

His aversion to Charlene increased by the minute and he was happy the beach house was locked up. He even hoped it would pour with rain next day so he could avoid walking along the beach, which he felt would contaminate his memories. He shuddered at the thought of going to their room after dinner.

The bedroom and bathroom were pink and white and Charlene giggled as she flopped down on the pink bedspread. He knew she expected him to lie next to her but instead he walked over to the window and looked out over the almost silent street below him.

He puffed softly through his lips, closed his eyes and wished he was home.

Charlene was in the pink bathroom when he turned around.

"Oh, what a cute bathroom", she cooed.

He wished she would stop using the word, 'cute'. He wanted to tell her to act her age, she was not seventeen. He knew the night was going to be a disaster and it would be his fault.

When he turned around Charlene was fluffing up bubbles in the bath. He knew she expected him to wash her back, work his way down her body, around her breasts and between her legs. Instead he stayed in the bedroom watching the late night news as though that was more important than satisfying his possibly nymphomaniac ex-girl friend.

She returned to the bedroom drying her hair and wearing the uninteresting T-shirt.

"I'm finished if you want the bathroom", she informed him, sounding worried and disappointed.

"Thanks", he replied, avoiding eye contact.

"Listen", she said. "It's all a little too quick, for me, for both of us. Shall we take things slowly".

Jack looked down at the pink carpet. "Sorry, it's my fault. Emy's death is too new. I thought I could sweep it away, get over it, but I can't, not yet. Perhaps in a little while".

"That's alright", she answered, sympathetically. "I understand. I'm tired. I think I'll call it a day".

"Yes, so will I. The traffic was heavy".

He felt mean, in fact he felt very guilty as though he had encouraged her when he knew full well it was not really what he wanted.

He removed a bedside table and pushed the twin beds together to soften the tension. Charlene smiled as though her damaged ego had been slightly repaired when he got into bed and turned on his side to face her. She smiled gently and he kissed her cheek and she returned mouthy kisses. His sexual needs took control for just a moment. Then he sat up.

"I can't, I don't have a condom".

"We don't need those", she whispered. "Nothing can go wrong at my age", she laughed, lightly.

"Yes, it can", he answered. "I always wear one".

He knew he sounded as though he slept around on a regular basis and that such a remark was suggesting one, or both, of them was possibly carrying a social disease.

Charlene sat up, horrified. "You know what, Jack Nielson, I don't know you and I have a feeling I don't want to. Perhaps you have too much baggage, too much past. How do I know where you've been and who with".

"I'm just careful".

"No, you're just insulting".

She got up and pushed her bed away from his while he walked across to the window to breathe in the fresh night air and look at the stars glittering in the dark blue sky. A butterfly resting on the windowsill flew up and fluttered around his head before disappearing. He did not know why but he thought of Emy.

"I love you, Emy. I will never forget you", he murmured, as he returned to his bed.

Charlene laid on her side with her back to him and he thought that was what he wanted. He had no need, at this moment, to live his youth again. He wanted only to concentrate on the years he had with Emy. He would return home and talk to Rosie. Maybe she could help to make him feel better. But first he had to help Jillie. She was coming home, she sounded upset. He sighed, he could hardly manage his own life let alone his daughter's. She needed a mother, she needed Emy, just like he did.

Emily Nielson found herself at the end of his bed. She did not know how she got there only that she was there. She had returned several times since she had died, it was as though she was allowed to sort things out. Recently, she had been able to enter Sophie's mind while she was under the shower, filling her with doubt while Mike waited for his night of love.

Now she was here with Jack. Love filled her soul as she stroked his hair and kissed his cheek with her thoughts.

He dreamt Emy was swimming towards him as a screeching sea gull flew overhead. He grabbed her wrist and kissed her as they both descended into the warm blue sea.

He woke with a start as a black shadow moved across the room.

"Emy?".

He looked up to see the butterfly resting on the pink lampshade above his bed.

"Don't leave", he whispered. "I need you".

*   *   *

JILLIE

Jack WAS SWEEPING LEAVES in the front garden when Jillie arrived in her old second hand car. He strolled towards her, smiling, for her visits were too short and too seldom.

She greeted him with a warm kiss as she made her way to the front door. Jack followed her, recognising how much she took after her mother, her movements, the way she held her head, the small side glance, the grin. Everyone said she looked like him but he could not see it. Still, she had inherited his blond hair and that was enough to satisfy him.

"Good you could make it. It's been too long since your last visit".

"I've been studying like mad. I might get a 'first' if I'm lucky. I have to make a decision about next year, whether to go on or not. I mean, what can I do with history, even a 'first' isn't going to find me a job".

"You don't know that".

"I think I do. I'm thinking about genealogy".

"That sounds interesting. Is there any work to be found in it".

"Probably not, but I'm going to look into it".

"Well, you can start with my side of the family. I mean the name Nielson must say something. Traces of an invading Viking who ravished some wild peasant girl".

"Possibly", she laughed. "But I doubt she would have known his name, if he had one. Maybe, he was known as 'Wilfred the Winner'.

"More likely 'Lars the Loser'. I think I'll change my name to Jack de l'Oser-Nielson.

She laughed again and threw her arms around his neck. "That's French not Scandinavian. Anyway, you're not a loser, never have been and never will be".

"I lost your mother. You can blame me for that".

He turned away, aware that he had never spoken like that before. He had actually spoken words he hardly dared to admit.

"Don't talk like that. It's not true. She had bad luck, really rotten bad luck. Anyway, talking of mum, I have something to tell you".

"What?", he asked, suddenly feeling nervous.

"Mum. I think I've seen her. I think I've spoken to her".

He felt a jolt pass through him, a basic human fear of the unknown.

"Impossible".

"Yes, I know it is. But something happened, something I can't account for".

"What?".

"I'll tell you while I make dinner. I've bought some fresh salmon steaks and I'm going to cook them with spring onions, lemon zest and juice and crème fraiche, together with pasta.

"I was sitting in the park, swotting up for an exam", she recounted after dinner as though she was about to tell him a story. "When a woman came and sat next to me. I didn't take much notice of her until she said how she had lived abroad. Well, I was polite and asked where and she replied Singapore. I told her how you and mum had been out there when you were young. Then, she said how she had two daughters, one from a first marriage. I thought that was a coincidence but not more than that.

Anyway, she went on to say how different they were from each other but, of course, they had two different fathers so that was to be expected. And then, and this is what did it, she said she had two friends, one had a cottage by a lake, the other by the sea. It was as though the wind was taken out of my sails.

And then she said something about our meeting being inevitable, that it had to happen. She got up to go and, of course, I also stood up. She took my arm and kissed me on the cheek, exactly as mum used to do, and said, 'you will never forget me, you will never forget today'.

And then she left. I should have watched where she went but, somehow, I could not do that".

Jack made a humming sound as he turned over the facts.

"Do you know what I think?".

"No, tell me".

"I think what she said could apply to anyone, most people know someone with a cottage somewhere, wherever. Most people kiss on the cheek and to say you will never forget her, well yes, that was clever of her. Of course, you will always remember her, she planted an idea in your head and it will stay there, forever. That's what I think".

"I am sure you're right, Pa, only is it not a coincidence that she lived in Singapore?".

"Thousands of Brits lived in Singapore. That is not so special".

"And having two daughters from different marriages?".

"Same difference".

"That photo, the one you took of Helen's lake".

"Yes, what about it?".

"Well, this woman told me about it. I mean, she can't have known there was one, not in a thousand years".

She wiped her hands on a dishcloth as she wandered into the lounge and stood studying the photo in a way she had never done before.

Her mother had told her how it was taken on a beautiful day, the willows were mirrored in the water and the sun had formed a beam which faded onto a nearby clearing. It was an unusual photograph.

She remembered how her mother had mixed emotions about going down to the cottage, about Helen, though she never really said what they were. It seemed something happened the day the photo was taken, something which upset her mother but, as always, she would not go into any details. She felt Helen had a great deal to answer for, if not everything.

"It all sounds very romantic. If you ask me, it's all coincidence. No more than that. Did she look like your mother?".

"No, I don't think so".

"Well, then, she wasn't. There's a good film on the telly tonight. Something historical, I believe".

"Fine, I'll clear up then we'll put our feet up and have a glass of wine. In vino veritas".

"In wine there is truth", he sighed.

"Perhaps I'll find the truth in a glass of plonk".

"I've tried that. It doesn't work. Next day, the truth is just a bloody headache".

She curled up in bed that night turning over the story she had told her father. He had scoffed at it, she had expected him to do so. It was no surprise. But still, as her father said, the woman had planted something in her mind, something she could not shake off. She felt it was not only what the woman had said but rather how she had said it. Her tone, the inclination of her voice, was familiar. She spoke how her mother would have spoken.

Ann Bailey

She knew she had a vivid imagination, her mother had always told her she was 'a pea in the pod'. She was so like her. She thought her mother understood all the strange quirks which she experienced as a small child and even later, though she seldom told her mother everything. Such as, how when her mother had enthused over the beach house, how lovely it was, the setting, the sea and sand, the gulls swooping overhead, she had only wanted to leave and made the excuse to go for a walk.

She did not like the beach house, it was wrong, perhaps haunted. She could remember coming down one Saturday afternoon after her mother had spent the night there by herself. She was pretty sure something had happened for her mother refused to be alone there again. After all, she was psychic, if there was anything to see, she would have seen it.

She crept downstairs to the bookcase in the lounge, Vici looked up and then went back to sleep. At least, he pretended he was asleep but, most probably, he was just laying with his eyes closed listening to her every movement. She was glad her father had taken him, it was company, it was safer.

She pulled a book off the shelf, stroked Vici and went back to bed. The book was one she had hardly ever opened, she thought it would make her feel guilty if she did, so she did not. She knew where to look for the information, it was not difficult to find. It was the gospel of St. Luke, Chapter 24.

She needed some form of confirmation that

there was a possibility for the dead not only to contact the living through thought, or even as an apparition, but through the flesh. It was not that she thought her mother was nearer to God, so to speak, but rather the fact that if it had been done once, perhaps it could be done again. Perhaps it was an everyday occurrence which no one knew about or recognised when it happened. Perhaps, she thought, the world was full of unrecognised people who were spirits incarnate, who appeared to give the living a message, to comfort the grieving, a memory of past love, to tease those who were too self assured. She even thought death could have a fun ending, there were so many people she would like to haunt, in a good way, of course.

She held the Bible tightly as she tried to sleep.

"I've been thinking", she said, after breakfast. "I want to stay on, try for a Masters. If I can afford it".

"You mean if I can afford it", Jack replied, emphasizing the 'I'.

"I've been offered a few hours at the local library. Got that through a friend. It's not much but perhaps I can get a few hours in a bar or café".

"Just do what you want. I'm not going anywhere and I don't seem to spend anything. I have never lived so cheaply, well not since I was a bachelor".

"Yes, women cost money", she laughed, lightly, not wanting to suggest her mother was an expensive woman but rather to warn him of any new love which might fall across his path.

"Your mother wasn't", he tried to laugh. "She really didn't ask for much. Just love".

He was surprised again at his openness, that was not like him. He thought maybe he needed to talk about Emy and who better than his girls. He thought he would ask Sophie and Tom down for the next bank holiday weekend. Perhaps they could all do something together.

"Can you come down for the Bank Holiday", he asked, hopefully. "I'm going to ask Sophie, if she can make it, I thought we could have a sort of family weekend".

"Super, it's time we got together. You know what we were talking about last night, well I want to go back to the park, once in a while. Maybe, she will return, then I can find out more about her".

"Don't waste too much time. It's what I said, if you say enough vague things some will fit. That's what she did. She probably goes around talking to people on park benches. Every now and again she hits the jackpot".

"You're probably right. Still I can just as well read a book on a park bench, if the weather is right, than in my rather dismal room".

"Of course", he agreed, picking up the Sunday newspaper.

"Do you want to talk about mum?"

He laid the newspaper on his lap.

"What is it you want to hear?".

"About the two of you, how you were together. What happened".

"I was faithful to your mother all my married life until".

"Until?".

"Until I got that stupid motorbike and had the feeling of wanting to relive my youth. Now it sounds so pathetic. A man my age rushing around the countryside trying to be twenty".

"I can understand that. I can understand life being dull, suffocating. I'm sure mum understood. She said she did".

"Everyone who loves another cares. I'm sure your mother cared. She hid it well, I must say".

"Perhaps she also enjoyed her freedom, ever thought about that?".

"Yes, of course, I realise that. But she didn't rush off on her bicycle, did she".

Jillie giggled. "She would have to do a hell of a lot of peddling to get very far. Though she did get to Devon".

Jack looked up surprised. "When did she go to Devon?".

Jillie blushed. "Oh, it was nothing. That man Sophie was running around with, he asked mum down to talk about he and Sophie getting hitched. She went but he didn't tell her, I guess he got cold feet. It's not important anymore".

"Who was he, again?".

"Some man called Montague".

"Oh, yes, now I remember. I didn't know she went down to see him", he muttered, sounding puzzled. "I wonder why she didn't tell me".

"See, we all have our secrets. I guess you

whizzing off made her feel she didn't have to tell you everything. I can understand that. Anyway, how did 'Helen the Horrid' fit in", she added, not trying to hide her dislike of the woman.

"She had been chasing me since kingdom come. I had a weak moment and I succumbed to kingdom come", he smiled at his rhyming.

"Did that cost mum her life?".

"Why do you say that?", he gasped.

"Because if Helen had not been around, mum would be alive today".

"We can't control everything", he muttered.

"You could have seen the consequences, if you had chosen to", she shouted.

Jack turned away.

"I'm sorry, I didn't mean that. It's just that there is so much unsaid, what really happened. Why you left mum upstairs alone. If you hadn't done that, she might still be alive", she sobbed as she ran upstairs, trying to hold back her tears. "And I don't give a damn what you think. It was mum I spoke to. I know it was her because she told me her dog had died recently in an accident. And for your information, I am going to look for her, everywhere I go I will look for her. At every bus stop, in every bar and restaurant, every supermarket I go to, I will look for her. I will find her and then", she stopped as she ran to her bedroom, sobbing.

Jack gave a deep sigh. It was true, he had never given a full account of that day. He could not and, so long as he need not, he would not. Neither would he ever reveal his last meeting with Helen or that he had an Hiv test. He had crawled through the eye of the needle and now he wanted to be quiet, to live simply, to allow himself to mourn Emy. To accept he had been undeserving of her love. Charlene had been a disaster, he had hoped loving her would lessen the pain. But it was not so, the idea of another love was out of the question, at least at this moment.

He made two cups of coffee and took them upstairs. Jillie was sitting on her bed watching television with a tissue in her hand.
"I have to take Vici for a walk. I was thinking of going to the 'Crossing'. I thought you might like to come with me. I have also something to tell you. You are not alone thinking you saw mum, you are not the first to see her".

*   *   *

LOVE IN THE MIST

It WAS A BEAUTIFUL APRIL DAY when he picked up the telephone. It was Poppy.

"How can I help you?", he asked, amused at hearing from the old lady.

"I told Will he would go and he has. Just walked away. I knew it when I saw him being picked up by the local florist".

"I take it you are talking about Arnold Waters".

"Yes, Arnie, of course. Will is smiling from ear to ear but the truth is we need help in the garden and goodness knows where else. You said you had nothing to do and you liked gardening".

He cleared his throat. "Well, yes, maybe for a short time, just to tide you over, if you can't find anyone else".

"Well, if you come along I'll show you what needs doing".

"When do you want me to come?", he sighed.

"Now", replied Poppy. "I need help now".

He looked at his cup of freshly made coffee next to the unread newspaper. He really did not need this.

"Can you give me an hour or two, I have first to take my dog out?".

"Fine, whatever you like. Do you want paying?", she added.

"Of course not". 'But I'm not stopping you', he thought.

"See you in an hour then", she replied, quickly, obviously frightened he might change his mind.

"Shit", he muttered, as he hung up.

He had been weeding flower beds for some hours before Poppy offered a beer along with a sandwich.

He stood straightening his back muscles before sitting down on one of the garden chairs, he thought he probably needed to go to a gym but he had little interest in that. Perhaps, he might still buy a small yacht and join the local club situated by a very medium sized lake. He had sneered at Emy's suggestion but now it all seemed such a bother to go too far afield. He would seriously think about it as life had ground to a standstill and Charlene was long gone. He was sorry about that but he felt nothing for her, she no longer appealed to him and he wondered what he had ever seen in her. Well, he probably did know, youth with an overdose of testosterone

"Jack", called Poppy. "I have someone who would like to meet you".

He looked up to see a middle aged woman standing next to Poppy. She was medium height, reddish brown hair, which he thought was probably not her real colour, well dressed and carefully made up.

"Jack, this is Nancy", Poppy stated. "She's from the States".

He stood up and held out his hand.

"Jack. My son is called Jack after my late husband's father. I just love that name", she spoke with a soft American accent.

"Are you on a visit?", he asked, politely, noting her inappropriate high heeled shoes.

"Yes, I'm staying with Aunt Poppy", she replied, smiling sweetly. "Aunt Poppy is one of my mother's sisters. My mother was the youngest of five girls. Can you imagine that, five girls?".

"No, not really, I've only got two and that's more than enough".

"I'll get you another beer", offered Poppy, sweetly. "Coffee", she stated, staring coldly at Nancy.

"What are your plans?", he asked.

"Well, I've already been to London, of course, and other places. I believe there are bus trips. I don't want to ask Poppy or Will, they are too busy to run me around. They said their season is just starting up but I didn't want to come in the winter. Everything is so dull then".

"Perhaps I can help you, show you around".

"That would lovely, how kind of you".

"Where do you come from?".

"Just across the pond. Maine".

"It must be beautiful there".

"Yes, it is. I am very fortunate. The sea is close and the children come up in the summer to sail".

"Do you sail?"

"Oh, yes. Whenever I can", she lilted.

"I used to sail. Actually, I'm on the point of buying a small yacht. Maybe, we can sail this summer", he suggested, enthusiastically.

"I would love that. Just say when. I'm not going anywhere".

"Neither am I".

Poppy arrived with the beer and coffee. "You won't believe it, Arnie's turned up. He said he hadn't left here at all. It was just a misunderstanding. He only took a few days off because he had pulled his back and was a bit tired. How about that!".

"Thank God", he sighed.

"Well, at least we met", Nancy, commented. "See something good came out of it".

Poppy gave a wry smile, which he was unable to interpret, and returned to the house.

"Have you ever been on the back of a motorbike?", he asked, foolishly, since he no longer knew what to say.

"Never and I have no wish to do so. I like my hair to stay in place".

"Quite right", he agreed.

Rosie suddenly appeared. "Jack Nielson, whatever are you doing", she asked, glancing at his boots and dirty hands.

"Having a drink with Nancy".

"I see you've met".

Jack frowned, her remark sounded more like a warning. He wondered whether their family ties were as amicable as Nancy had implied.

"Nancy, is going back home next week. Aren't you, dear?", she said, sounding very sure that was so.

"Am I, so soon?".

"Yes, you're flying back next Tuesday. You've been here three weeks already, we've done a lot of sightseeing", she said kindly. "London twice, Stratford-on-Avon, Stonehenge, Bath, numerous country houses. In fact, Will and I have been pretty busy running you around".

"It went so quickly", Nancy replied, sounding sad.

"I'll be getting back to the weeding", he said, clearing his throat as he walked towards the flower beds.

"You don't have to do that, I don't know what got into Poppy asking you to work here and what with she and Nancy bickering all the time".

"I see Nancy has a problem".

"Yes, two of her children are divorced and both are living with her. She has to go back next week but she's enjoyed herself so much she doesn't want to go. Sad really, I wish I could help her".

"If you had asked me sooner, I would have taken her around for you".

"Well, next time. There's always a next time. Nothing stays the same for long", she mumbled as she walked back to Nancy.

He finished off the flower bed and was on the point of taking the tools back to the garden shed when a slightly built man approached him, followed by young woman.

"I'm Arnold Waters", he said, holding out his hand. "I've just heard that Poppy roped you in, sorry about that. This is Alison, my daughter".

He shook her hand. It was a noticeably firm handshake.

"I've just finished", he informed her, looking down at the flower bed. "I've thinned them out".

"Oh, you shouldn't have done that. They're 'Love in the Mist'. They always look a bit straggly".

"Appropriate name", he chuckled. "That just about sums it up. Love, I mean".

He turned away embarrassed at his comment.

Alison laughed. "I know all about it. I walked around in a haze for some time. When it cleared, I found myself at sea".

"Very good. That says it all. I'm still battling the storm", he chuckled at their repartee.

He thought Alison blushed a little.

"Well, I have to get to work. I'm helping dad, he pulled his back but he won't lie down", she explained.

"Have no time to do nothing, Alison. Now, if you begin to plant out, I'll bring the hose pipe", Arnie butted in, hoping to break up their convivial chatter.

"I like gardening, it's about the only thing I do reasonably well. It's my only hobby", he informed her.

Ann Bailey

"It's my work", she grinned. "This is how I earn my bread and butter".

"I can think of worse ways. Do you live around here?".

"Yes, in the village with my dad. He and my mother divorced. She went up to Yorkshire to visit her sister and never came back. It's okay, dad's happy, mum's happy. What more is there to say".

"What about you?".

"No one has ever asked me that. Good question, I'll have to think about that one".

She sat on the ground and took out a cigarette.

"Dad needs me. He is sometimes a bit wobbly, if you know what I mean. He belongs to a spiritual club, meditation and all of that.

He's what you call 'sensitive'. For example, he thinks the rockery is essential for the balance of energy. People find him strange which rather isolates him. Some people even think he is 'on the other side' but he isn't. He's just not macho".

"He doesn't have to be, everyone is different".

"He thinks he sees spirits, actually I think he does. He was just saying the other day how he once in a while sees a woman sitting on the bench by the 'Crossing'. She has a dog with her".

Jack looked stunned. "What kind of dog?".

"I don't know, I'll ask him. Does that say anything to you?".

"No, of course not. I'm just interested. That's all. Where do you work?", he asked, wanting to change the subject.

"I help dad. He owns 'The Nursery'. At the moment, he's tied up with Feng Shui and Bonsai. I'm slowly replacing him".

"He is good at what he does", Jack answered, looking around the garden. "Well, I guess I had better be off".

"I think I've seen you at 'The Nursery', though not recently", she rushed her remark, as though trying to keep the conversation going a little longer.

"Yes, I used to go a lot. Not so much anymore, since I lost my wife".

"Yes, Rosie told me about it. I'm sorry".

He turned as he heard a sound on the stones between the flower beds.

"Still here?", asked Rosie, slightly out of breath.

"Yes, I've been talking to Alison".

"Alison is my surrogate daughter, aren't you dear?".

Alison reddened. "If you say so", she giggled.

"I don't have any children and she seldom sees her mother. What more can I ask for?".

"I've a couple of daughters you can adopt, Rosie. I can see you've made a good choice".

Alison lowered her head. "Thanks for that. All admiration kindly received and accepted. Shall we form a mutual admiration society?".

"Good idea, but you'll have a job finding something to admire", he replied, sounding sad.

"Would the two of you like to come to supper", Rosie asked, quickly, sensing Jack's unhappiness. "Poppy is making a 'Toad in the Hole'.

Would you like to try it out? Nancy will be there. That should liven things up".

"I would love to", answered Alison, not looking at Jack.

"Thanks, fine. Can I just go home to let the dog out. He's been alone for sometime".

"I'll walk with you, I'll just get Megan. She's in the house, probably being spoilt by Poppy".

"Megan?".

"My dog, she comes everywhere with me".

Jack stood almost frozen with disbelief as they entered the conservatory. Megan was sitting on Poppy's lap being pampered. She was a small black poodle.

Alison picked her up and ruffled the soft curly hair on her head.

"She's beautiful. I wasn't planning to take a poodle but I couldn't resist her. I got her from the local dog's home".

"That's where I got Vici. I hope he behaves himself, he could make mincemeat of her", he said, sounding worried.

"Don't you worry about Megan. She's a girl who can hold her own and, if not, then I'll carry her. It's such a lovely afternoon to walk across the heath. We can sit on the bench when we get back and see if we can call up dad's lady friend, the spirit and her dog".

He winced but Alison did not notice. Why should she.